Marge

The Collection

9 stories in 1

ISLA FISHER

Illustrated by Eglantine Ceulemans

Picca
PRE

The edition first published in Great Britain in 2018 by
PICCADILLY PRESS
80–81 Wimpole St, London W1G 9RE
www.piccadillypress.co.uk

Marge in Charge first published in Great Britain 2016
Marge and the Pirate Baby first published in Great Britain 2017
Marge and the Great Train Rescue first published in Great Britain 2017

A CIP catalogue record for this book is available from the British Library.

ISBN: 978-1-84812-797-5
also available as an ebook

1

Printed and bound by Clays Ltd, Elcograf S.p.A.

Piccadilly Press is an imprint of Bonnier Zaffre Ltd,
part of Bonnier Books UK
www.bonnierbooks.co.uk

For Olive, Elula and Monty,
my favourite small people on the planet
and the best editors a writer could wish for,
for my mum and dad, who are more
fun than any wacky babysitter,
and for my grandmother Anna,
who taught me to love books.

CONTENTS

Marge
Babysits

My name is Jemima Button. I am seven years old and I'm the tallest girl in my class. My little brother is Jakeypants, though grown-ups call him Jake, and he is four years old. He loves wrestling, dinosaurs and ice cream.

We live with our mummy and daddy in an ordinary house, on an ordinary street. We used to be an ordinary family until the day our babysitter came.

It was five o'clock on Thursday, and our family was sitting around the table. Our parents were dressed up in their smart clothes.

'Why do we need a babysitter?' asks Jake.

'Because we are going out for dinner,' explains Daddy, patting Jakeypants on the head.

Mummy smiles and says, 'We need someone here to look after you.'

I can see that my baby brother is not happy. He begins to cry – well, fake cry. He wails and flails his arms around like a baby penguin on slippery ice.

'Do you want to read a story?' asks Daddy, handing Jake his favourite book.

'Stupid book!' says Jake and throws it on the ground.

Oh no. I bite my lip. When Jakeypants starts throwing things it means he is headed for a tantrum. What will our new babysitter think? The last time we had a babysitter Jake spent the whole time hiding in his room building a Lego weapon so that he could 'destroy' her! He was cross at her because she scolded him for covering Daddy's desk with stickers. And then I had to peel them all off!

I hope Jakey behaves himself tonight. He can be very stubborn and naughty when he wants to be.

'There's your favourite for dinner: macaroni cheese,' says Mummy, as she puts it into the fridge. Jake's face lights up, but not for long.

'. . . and broccoli,' he adds, scowling. 'I don't want broccoli and I definitely do NOT want a babysitter,' Jake shouts.

'Even if the broccoli is on your blue T. rex plate?' Mummy pleads.

'Especially then!' Jakey retorts.

Mummy gives Daddy a panicked look.

Everyone knows that my little brother has two rules:

1. He won't wash his hair — he says it's 'boring'

2. He won't eat broccoli. Ever

But then we meet someone extraordinary: our new babysitter.

DING DONG, that's the doorbell.

Straight away Jakey stops crying and races to the door. He peeks through the window then takes off his shorts and pulls them over his head. Jake always does this when he wants to wrestle or stop someone from coming in the house, like Uncle Desmond.

'Put your shorts back on,' Mummy says sternly. Daddy is opening the door.

'Meet Marge!' Daddy says in the voice he saves for his boss at work.

I peep from behind Daddy as I always feel shy around new grown-ups.

There she is – Marge, the babysitter!

Standing in our hallway is a person so small that she only comes up to Daddy's armpit! She is wearing a little yellow woolly hat and reading glasses.

Her face looks serious too and I worry that she will be strict, like my nursery teacher Mrs Ratley, who made us eat all our packed lunch even when the sandwiches were soggy.

She has a big round belly and skinny legs with knees as knobbly as twigs.

'Hi, Marge,' I say and give her my bravest smile.

But Jake has only noticed how small Marge is. She is definitely NOT tall enough to ride a rollercoaster. She could even fit in Jake's cardboard box that he uses as his superhero hideout.

'Are you a kid or a grown-up?' he asks, peering closely at her.

'Definitely a grown-up,' answers Marge gleefully.

'Then why are you so small?' demands Jake.

'Well, why are YOU so small?' asks Marge right back.

'Because I'm only four years old!' Jake rolls his eyes. He is brilliant at eye rolling even though Mummy told him that it's rude to do it to grown-ups. 'You look one hundred years old,' he snorts.

Mummy and Daddy look worried that Marge will be offended but instead she throws her head back and laughs. This makes me feel a little bit less nervous, so I say, 'I'm Jemima.'

'Nice to meet you,' Marge says solemnly, shaking my hand like adults do. It makes me giggle.

'Are you a Christmas elf?' asks Jake. 'Let me see if your ears are pointy.' Jake is now peering at the sides of Marge's head. Daddy coughs nervously and steers Jake away from Marge.

'The rules are on the fridge,' Mummy tells Marge. 'If you have any questions ask Jemima, she's my big girl. We will be back by eight o'clock.' Then she turns to us. 'Remember to be polite and say "please" and "thank you" when Marge takes care of you.'

'We will,' I promise.

I hear Mummy telling Marge that it's very important for Jake to eat all his dinner, especially the broccoli, and wondering if she could possibly try washing his hair? Then she gives Marge the number of her mobile phone for emergencies.

Mummy and Daddy both give me a big hug. The butterflies in my belly aren't so fluttery now that we've met Marge. I am very curious about her, but still nervous that my little brother might misbehave.

To my surprise, though, he lets Mummy hug him goodbye, which he never normally does.

We stand on the doorstep either side of Marge and wave as my parents leave. The minute the car has gone, we head inside.

'Are you a dwarf? From *Snow White*?' Jakey asks.

'No, and I'm not an Oompa-Loompa either,' laughs Marge.

'Oompa-Loompas only exist in *Charlie and the Chocolate Factory*,' I say.

'Are you a jockey? Do you gallop horses in a race?' Jake asks.

Marge shakes her head.

'Did you drive here? How did your little feet reach the pedals?' asks Jake.

'I am sure you can lower the steering wheel!' I offer helpfully.

'I actually use a booster chair,' Marge says.

Then she leans in secretively.

'Being small means I can visit the museum half price!' she brags as she takes off her glasses and pea-green coat. Then Marge pulls off her hat. Guess what's underneath? Long colourful hair that falls halfway down her back! Green, blue, orange, red and yellow hair like a waterfall of colour.

I wonder if Mummy would let Marge look after us if she saw her crazy hair!

'Wow!' I say. Marge crosses her feet underneath her and exhales.

'I was born Margery Beauregard Victoria Ponterfois, and I am a duchess.'

'A duchess?' I ask, blinking. 'Are you Dutch?'

Marge laughs, and little creases form beside her blue eyes.

'No. The King of England's fourth son is my uncle Leonard.'

'Do you have any children?' I ask.

Marge shakes her head.

'But I have ten pets: three white miniature ponies, three swans, two polka-dot Pomeranian puppies, a cheeky long-tooth ferret and an albino water buffalo.'

I can barely breathe with excitement.

'I used to live at the palace but the royal guards wouldn't allow my pets to sleep in my bed. Did you know that there are 779 rooms at the royal palace? I was always getting lost. Sometimes I would fall asleep looking for my bedroom! So my pet friends and I set out on an adventure to find a new home.'

NORTH POLE: Alfie, Alvin & Arnoldo the swans are not happy with new home: too cold.

Jakey is behaving really well and I can tell that he's enjoying Marge's story.

'Have you ever been on a bus?' Jakey asks. He is obsessed with buses.

'Of course,' sniffs Marge. 'I have ridden a red double decker bus, an airport bus and a minibus . . .'

WOW! Jakey is really impressed with Marge now.

' . . . but my favourite mode of transport is the royal coach pulled by eight palomino donkeys.'

I want to ask Marge all sorts of questions about her animal friends and her life, but suddenly she jumps up and says: 'Now, your mummy wants me to read the rules on the fridge. Hop to it!'

We follow her to the kitchen, and Marge reads the list aloud:

1. Dinner is at 5.30. There's macaroni cheese and broccoli in the fridge

2. Playtime next but all toys must be put away afterwards

3. Bath time is at 6.30 and please try to wash Jake's hair

4. Bed by 7.30

I would much rather listen to more of Marge's story, but Marge is looking very serious now that she has read Mummy's list. 'I think we might need to add a few new dinner rules,' she says.

Jake groans, and my stomach sinks.

'I won't eat broccoli. Not now, not ever,' says my brother haughtily.

Marge just raises one eyebrow and she grabs a napkin and folds it. 'I have been to many exotic dinners all around the world. I have dined with princesses, knights, lords and ladies and I have my own royal dinner-making rules,' says Marge as she finishes crafting the napkin into a splendid chef's hat and pops it onto her own head.

Jake and I exchange an excited look. Cooking? Our new babysitter is going to let us cook! I race to the bottom drawer and find our aprons. We quickly put them on and tie the bows.

'Right, let's see . . .' says Chef Marge. '. . . Rule One: prepare the food. Jemima, you will be the chef's helper.' I have no idea what that is but I begin gathering all the ingredients that Marge tells me to and Marge informs Jakey that he will be the waiter.

'Do waiters get to wrestle?' Jake karate kicks the air.

'Yes. But first they have to ask the dinner party guests what they want for dinner and write it down in this little pad.' She hands a notebook and a silver pen to Jake.

'But I can't write any words yet – except for my name,' Jake sighs.

'Don't worry,' says Marge, 'I read squiggles! I can even read the handwriting of all my pets – how else do you think we communicate?'

WOW! I have always wondered whether chickens could handwrite, or rather claw-write.

'It all started when my camel asked me to translate a love letter she had received from a dairy cow. Now that was tough, because cows don't use their hooves for writing . . .'

'What do they use then?' asks
Jake curiously.

'Their tails, of course!' cries Marge. Then she gives Jakey and me a bowl. 'You know, Prince Leonard won the heart of my aunt with a red velvet birthday cake. Baron Dinklestitch wasn't pleased, mind you . . .'

Jake and I crack eight eggs into a bowl. Jakey accidentally drops in half of the shell but we just cover it in a pile of flour. Then we add a mountain of cereal and a teabag for good measure. Marge tells us she thinks that we are very creative chefs but I am not sure that Mummy would agree with that.

Once everything is cooking nicely Marge gets the list out again and adds another new rule.

Rule Two: lay the table.

Jake groans. But Marge tells us it's the only way to decide on our guest list for the dinner party.

'You mean we're inviting guests to eat with us?' I ask.

'Of course!' she replies. 'Dinner should always be a dinner party, and the perfect number for a dinner party is six.'

So we decide to include Archie, our pug-nosed puppy dog, but we still only have four!

'We will lay the table for six anyway and maybe some special guests will surprise us,' Marge says.

We place three plates and three forks and knives for every guest but because Archie can't use cutlery I give him a pair of chopsticks.

'What's next on Mummy's list?' I ask Marge, hoping she'll have some more extra rules.

Marge toots a pretend trumpet.

... Rule Three: decorate the dining room!

Soon we are cutting out cardboard stars and making streamers and Jake staples the stars onto the tablecloth. Then he gets carried away and staples his T-shirt to his shorts and staples one of his socks to a tea towel, and he is about to actually staple Archie's tail to his leg when Marge swoops in.

'Can I borrow the stapler?' Marge asks quickly and then hides it instantly.

Jake sticky tapes Pete, his toy stegosaurus, to the centre of the table as a decoration and we tie a ribbon on the back of everyone's chair. I only just learned how to tie a bow and I can do it quite quickly now.

'A room fit for kings and queens!' Marge says and high fives us both. 'And perfect for a duchess. It's all ready for dinner now.'

PHEW! My tummy is making funny grumbly sounds and I can smell our cake baking in the kitchen but then Marge checks the list again.

'It's time to get cleaned up so we can look fabulous for our dinner party,' Marge says, blowing the whistle hard. 'Bathtime!'

Bathtime before supper? This is very unusual but Marge is in charge, so we follow her upstairs.

In the bathroom Jake refuses to run the bath or fetch his towel. I am worried because I know how stubborn my little brother can be, but Marge has a fun idea. She fills the sink with water all the way to the top, and empties in a *whole* bottle of lavender bubble bath. It's incredible – bubbles are floating serenely onto the floor and covering our toes.

Then she tips in a bottle of apple shampoo,

Daddy's aftershave, Mummy's face cream and she even sprays in some fancy perfume.

Jakey holds his nose 'Phew-eee,' he says, giggling.

Then she somehow finds our swimming goggles, which have been lost for ages, and we put them on. Marge has a whistle. 'It's time to dunk!' she cries, blowing the whistle hard. 'One, two, three –

DUNK!'

Jakey and I plunge our heads in the sink and under the taps, then up again. Soon we are surrounded by bubbles floating under our chins and around our ears! Jakey makes a white Santa beard and I make a white wig of foamy bubbles.

'Shall we wash the dog too?' Marge says and I can hear her spraying more air freshener around the room. I can't even see her any more through all the bubbles.

'No,' I say firmly. Archie hates the water and will only go in the pond at the heath if he's chasing a ball.

'But didn't the list say we need to wash Archie's fur?'

'No,' I say, 'Mummy wrote Jake's hair, not Archie's fur!'

I'm feeling nervous again – but this time it's not about Jakey misbehaving. I'm worried that we might not get through the things on Mummy's list on time.

Suddenly Marge pops her head through

the bubbles and grins at us before turning to Jake. 'Do you want a shampoo mohican?'

Jake nods, although neither of us even know what a mohican is! Marge lathers up Jake's hair with shampoo until it stands in one point on top of his head. He looks hilarious, like a white rooster. Then she lathers up mine like an ice cream.

The bathroom is a bit of a mess, but Jake has clean hair and is happy and Mummy will be so happy too! I'm a bit worried, though – we've still got lots to do, and we haven't been following the list in order!

'What's this shelf?' Marge asks. I can vaguely see through the white fluffy clouds of foam that she has found Mummy's 'out-of-our-reach' shelf.

She unscrews a large pot of something sticky and brown and rubs it all over her face.

'This must be a mud mask, to tighten the pores of the skin,' Marge assumes. But I can read the label and it clearly says BROWN HAIR DYE.

Oh no! Marge has put hair dye all over her face. It's turning orange . . . She really does look like an Oompa-Loompa now!

'Quick, Marge, wipe it off!' I shout. 'That is not a face mask!'

I don't want Marge's face to be the same colour as Mummy's hair!

WHOOPEE! Marge plunges her face into the water in the sink and is scrubbing her cheeks! Now bubbles and water are all over the floor.

Archie trots into the bathroom and starts barking at Marge.

'I am Marge the Mermaid!' gurgles Marge as she pops back up.

'I told you she wasn't a real grown-up,' Jake whispers to me, looking around at the messy bathroom.

'Come on, Marge,' I say. 'It's time to get back to our list.'

I have to say it isn't easy finding Marge in those bubbles. They're everywhere, rising all the way up to the ceiling.

'Gotcha!' I say, grabbing her foot, but

31

then I lift it up and it's a bottle of shampoo!

'I have her elbow!' Jakey shouts and then holds up a bag of bath salts.

We both crack up laughing!

'Marge, is that you?' I say, pulling out a tub of body gel.

Finally I feel something moving and grab at her. She feels very hairy and furry and as I pull her out I realise I have Archie in my arms! How did Archie get into the sink?

'Boo!' shouts Marge through a curtain of foam, grinning from ear to ear.

Once we are dry, Marge has a new idea. 'What shall we wear to dinner?' she asks us, as if we are in charge, not her.

'Anything but shorts!' shouts Jake, his hair now clean and dry. Jakey HATES shorts. Even in summer.

'We can't wear ordinary clothes,' says
our babysitter. 'Going to a dinner party is
a regal affair and we have to look our best.'

I have an idea. 'I'll be right back!' I say
and I run off to find our dressing-up box.
When I get back I find Marge and Jakey in
Mummy and Daddy's room.

They are standing right inside Mummy's closet, pulling out all her special evening gowns. Oh no! Mummy will not be happy if we make a mess and I don't want to get in trouble. But it does look like fun . . .

'You can borrow my fairy wings,' I offer Marge. 'And my ladybird Halloween costume will fit Jakey.'

Marge shakes her head and instead she puts on a pirate patch and gladiator sword.

'At a dinner party it's important that you stand out,' says Marge, buttoning Jake into a yellow sequinned jacket. 'I was at a dinner party in Paris when I caught the eye of the Earl of Toulouse and he taught me to tango.'

'What's tango?' Jake is squinting at Marge.

'I'll show you,' says Marge and she picks

my little brother up into a hug and dances him around the room, singing loudly.

'The Earl Of Toulouse taught me to dance like this but he had a rose between his teeth and a red monkey jacket on.' Marge looks giddy with the memory.

Jake and I catch each other's eyes as Marge warbles on and start laughing so much my chest hurts. Then I remember Mummy has a pink feather boa. It's really soft and silky and she lets me wear it if I am very careful.

It would look perfect with Marge's hair so I find the box and offer it to her.

'You should wear it,' says Marge kindly.

I finally choose a sparkly evening gown and tall heels to go with the feather boa. I also wear Mummy's gold bracelets looped over my ears – Marge says I look like a baroness. Jake matches Daddy's wellington boots with his sequinned jacket and a French beret.

Marge grabs Daddy's black dinner jacket and folds up the sleeves to fit her short arms. And she adds the suit trousers which are so long they drag along the ground. She even finds his black bow tie and a top hat. Then she grabs a black magic marker from her handbag and draws a twirly-whirly moustache on her face. Marge looks like a boy!

'Moustaches make gentlemen look mysterious!' she says, bowing and talking in a deep voice.

Marge and I admire ourselves in Mummy's large mirror and pretend we are on our way to a swish restaurant, until we are distracted by the noise of Jakey jumping dangerously fast off Mummy's bed.

'That looks fun!' says Marge, and she joins in.

Soon we are all jumping off the bed and I finally understand why Jakey does it all the time.

My legs are so tired they are wobbly and my tummy is really rumbling when Marge holds out the list and sings, 'It's time for the dinner party to commence!'

'Who are the special guests?' Jakey wants to know.

As we walk downstairs, I am struck by an utterly brilliant idea. I sneak back to my bedroom and return with a shoebox that has holes poked in the top.

'Ta-da!' I cry.

I lift the lid.

'Marge, meet Bill and Bob: our pet snails. They can be our special dinner guests!'

Marge looks very pleased and Jake is jumping up and down with excitement.

'Mummy says they have to stay in the box, but this is a special occasion and we need six guests,' I reason, lifting them out gently.

'They leave a shimmery trail behind them like gooey fairy dust!' Jakey marvels.

'Now we have our guests, we can start!' Marge says with a cheer.

Marge carries Archie to Jakey's old highchair and he sits there looking quite confused.

He is not normally even allowed to be in the dining room and now he is sitting at the table with two chopsticks in front of him!

Jake takes everyone's orders very politely, gives his notepad to Marge, then sits quietly in his chair. I have never seen him so well behaved or with such clean hair. If only Mummy could see him now!

There are a lot of banging and crashing sounds in the kitchen before Marge brings out one large bowl covered by a silver lid.

I'm really hungry now so I'm quite excited.

Marge lifts the lid dramatically and underneath there is a big bowl of brown goo and six spoons.

'Chef Marge has your starter!'

'I am *not* eating *that*!' Jakey says. He's looking a little bit grumpy – I think he might be hungry too.

'It's *Soup a la Chocolatay*,' Marge announces in a perfect French accent.

'It's not the hair dye again, is it?' I ask.

Our babysitter digs her spoon daintily into the 'soup' before taking a big SLURRRP from her bowl.

'It's chocolate soup,' she says proudly. 'I melted three whole bars, and five mini ones that I found in my handbag.'

Chocolate soup?

'Mummy never lets us eat chocolate unless it's a special treat,' I explain. Jake and I exchange a grin.

'Marge is in charge,' says Jake cheerfully as he spoons some chocolate soup into his mouth. I have never seen Jake eat anything with a spoon before – he normally uses his fingers.

My tummy is rumbling and the melted

chocolate smells delicious so I pick
up a spoon and have a taste.

'Scrummy yummy in my tummy!'
I say. That's what Grandpa Bert always
says when he tastes anything delicious.

It's so tasty that before we know it Marge,
Jakey and I are hugging the bowl between
us and licking the inside and our fingers,
and chocolate is everywhere and Marge
tells us that unfortunately there isn't enough
left for the other guests at the dinner party.

Oops! I forgot about our dinner guests.
Bill and Bob have sloped away but Archie
looks disappointed.

Marge goes back to the kitchen to get the
next bit of the meal.

It feels like she is gone for a really long
time and we are really hungry now.

Finally Marge returns with pasta. 'And

now for our main course!' she announces. It's dripping with the white cheese sauce which we both love.

Marge shows Jake and I which fork to use and how to look elegant while eating pasta. We twizzle and whirl our forks and listen to Marge. She tells us a story about when she was young and the Queen of England taught her to use cutlery for the first time.

Archie does not look elegant as he wolfs down his portion of pasta – there is cheese sauce all over his face. He licks it off.

SLURP! SLURP!

'And now for dessert,' says Marge after we have finished. She disappears into the kitchen and although I'm quite full now I can't wait to eat more delicious food.

But Marge has a surprise in store – she returns with two small bowls of broccoli.

Jake shakes his head suspiciously. 'That is NOT dessert. That is broccoli and I refuse to eat it!'

'You are right, it is broccoli,' says Marge, smiling. 'And we can't eat broccoli at the dinner table,' she adds.

What is she thinking? Eating our dinner was the first rule on Mummy's list.

'We can't eat broccoli ANYWHERE,' says Jake crossly.

'What about on a bus?' Marge asks innocently. 'Would you eat broccoli on a bus?' Jakey's eyes widen as Marge drags over the cardboard box that he uses as his superhero hideout. She pulls four tiny chairs out from the playroom and puts them in two rows in the box, just like the inside of a bus!

Then she crawls inside the box and squeezes into the driver's seat!

'All aboard the bus, please,' she calls.

Jakey mimes giving Marge his ticket, then races inside the box and takes a seat happily. I bring over our bowls and sit down next to my brother. I nibble on my broccoli and pretend to wave out of the bus window.

Would you believe it, Jakey eats all his broccoli! Mummy will be thrilled.

Not only has Jake eaten his broccoli but he's used a fork and a spoon and his hair is clean.

Marge looks happy too as she checks everything off the list and sighs.

'After a royal banquet or dinner party, the guests retire into the living room to chat,' Marge explains. She curls up in Daddy's armchair.

Jakey and I snuggle up on the sofa. I don't even mind when Jakey leans his head on me.

'Don't you miss the palace?' I ask. I saw the changing of the guards at Buckingham Palace once, and I would love to go inside.

'Never!' retorts Marge. 'I left to travel the world seeking wild adventures in faraway lands!'

'Have you ever babysat before?' I ask.

'No. I am usually very, incredibly, always, typically . . . busy,' Marge replies with a yawn.

'What do you do for a job?' Jakey asks.

'Well, I try to take my puppies roller-skating every day, my ferret has an enormous hat collection and insists on trying them all on each morning and my ponies like me to tell them stories while braiding their tails – and those are only half of my jobs,' says Marge sleepily.

It's getting dark outside and I realise that it's probably past our bedtime, and Mummy and Daddy will soon be home. I think about the messy kitchen, Mummy's closet and the bathroom full of bubbles. Marge notices my expression. She looks tired.

'The cleaner will be here shortly, I'm sure.'

'Er, Marge . . .' I don't know how to break it to her. 'Marge – we don't have a cleaner!'

'What about a maid?' Marge asks, yawning.

I shake my head, no.

'A butler?' Marge's eyelids are drooping.

Again, I shake my head.

'Not even a chambermaid?' she mumbles sleepily.

'No,' I say. I don't even know what a chambermaid is!

But Marge has fallen asleep. Her skinny legs are poking out from underneath her belly as it rises and falls with each snore.

I check the clock and it's five to eight. Uh-oh. We are going to be in *big* trouble. My stomach feels quivery.

'Jake, we only have five minutes till Mummy and Daddy come back!' I whisper, so as not to wake our babysitter.

Jake jumps up in shock.

'We have to clean everything up or Mummy and Daddy won't let Marge come and look after us again!'

My little brother is looking at me with big worried eyes. 'Let's tidy, NOW!' he whispers back urgently.

I can't believe it because Jakey HATES tidying up! He must really like our new babysitter.

We rush from room to room like little whirlwinds. The whole house is a disaster zone. There are towels and bubbles on the bathroom floor, Mummy's clothes are thrown around the living room and the kitchen sink is piled up with chocolatey bowls. Marge is still fast asleep in Daddy's armchair. Her messy rainbow hair is spread out and she still has a black marker moustache and chocolate around her mouth.

Gently I wake her up. 'Marge, it's time to clean your face and brush your hair before Mummy and Daddy get back. We'll tidy the house.' She smiles sleepily at me and shuffles off towards the downstairs toilet.

Then I run around picking up Mummy's clothes while Jake grabs the mop and starts on the bathroom floor. I rinse the dishes and leave them in a sink full of hot, bubbly water. Jake puts Mummy's make-up away and I manage to make the dining room look normal again by tossing all our decorations into the laundry basket.

'Marge?' I call, wondering if she's finished getting ready. But she doesn't reply and I can't see her anywhere downstairs – our babysitter has disappeared!

There's no time to find her – I can hear Mummy and Daddy at the front door.

Quickly, we bolt upstairs to our bedroom. Archie is curled up sleeping on the rug in our room. Whyever is he not sleeping in his own doggy bed? I scramble onto my top bunk and Jakey flings himself onto the bottom bunk just as Mummy creaks opens our bedroom door.

I give a snorting sound which I hope Mummy will think is a snore.

Mummy and Daddy kiss our faces softly as we pretend to be sleeping.

'They're fast asleep,' she whispers to Daddy.

I hear them move towards the door.

'Is that Bob on the table?' she asks.

I open an eye. Oh no!

'Oh, and there's Bill,'
says Dad. 'They must have
got loose, but how did they get upstairs?'

Mum picks up Bob and Bill and puts them into their shoebox before tiptoeing out of our bedroom.

The door closes quietly.

I wait a minute and then, leaving Jake snuggled in bed, sneak out onto the landing and peek through the bars of the staircase and down into the living room. To my surprise Marge is standing in the hallway, wide awake, with a clean face, and looking sensible with all her magical hair hidden away!

I peer closer and see Archie's green

blanket stuck to Marge's back like a cape.

That's why we couldn't find her – Marge must have crept off to sleep in Archie's doggy bed!

I snort back a giggle. I guess being small can be useful when it comes to finding comfy places to nap!

'How were they?' Daddy asks.

'The kids ate all their dinner, even the broccoli, and Jake's hair is clean,' Marge says proudly.

'Thank you!' Mummy says happily.

'It was easier washing my albino water buffalo's tail than Jake's hair though,' Marge says seriously, but Mummy and Daddy laugh, thinking that she is making a joke.

Jake and I both know that she's not!

When I'm back in our room I wriggle under my covers and sigh in wonder.

'Are you awake, Jakey?' I ask.

'Almost,' he says sleepily.

'Do you think Marge is a real duchess?' I ask.

Jake doesn't answer for a long time. Then I hear a giggle.

'Yes.'

'Why are you laughing?' I ask.

'We have a royal babysitter,' he says. 'But we have to babysit her!'

Jake's right, and it makes me smile. 'I hope that she comes again,' I reply, snuggling into my pillow.

Jake and I are silent, thinking about it for a moment.

'Do you think Mummy would buy me some rainbow hair dye? Jakey, what do you think?' I ask.

But there is only the soft sound of his breathing.

'Night-night, Jakey,' I whisper, and I turn out my light and drift off to sleep.

Marge at the Birthday Party

Hi! Remember me? I'm Jemima Button. I am seven years old and still the tallest in my class – though Rosie Williams is catching up with me now.

It's nine o'clock on Saturday morning. Jakey and I are downstairs eating eggs and soldiers. Jake is secretly feeding our puppy Archie all the runny yellow part of the egg, which he calls the 'yuk' instead of the 'yolk'. I have finished mine and now I'm drawing a picture of Granny's tabby cat George, who looks like an old man with a yellow beard.

Today I have butterflies in my tummy because Marge, our amazing babysitter, is taking us to Theo's party. Theo is Jake's best friend from school. He has one long eyebrow and always shares his snacks with Jake. Even though I am very excited to see Marge, I won't know anyone at the party, I will be the oldest child there and possibly the only girl! What if no one plays with me?

Mummy and Daddy can't come because they have to drive a long way today to visit Auntie Sally, who has had a new little baby. I'd love to meet baby Zara but I get carsick.

'Are you two going to be on your best behaviour for Marge today?' asks Daddy.

Jake and I share a hidden smile and nod our heads.

We can't promise that Marge will be on her best behaviour! She always seems sensible until Mummy and Daddy leave and then we end up having so much fun and making up our own rules to add to Mummy's list. Marge is secretly a duchess who used to live in a huge royal palace. But she hung up her tiara to live a life of incredible adventures. Anyway, she couldn't fit all her extraordinary pets into the palace stables!

DING DONG
Marge is here!

We jump up and run for the door.

Jakey beats me there and pulls it open. Our babysitter smiles from the doorstep.

'Look, I had a splinter yesterday!' cries my little brother. He lifts up his foot for Marge to see the scratch on his heel. 'Daddy took it out with tweezers and I didn't even cry,' he brags.

'Very brave,' says Marge, pinching his chubby cheeks. Jake never allows anyone else to do that!

Today Marge looks even smaller than I remembered. Can grown-ups shrink? She's wearing a smart jacket, stripy leggings and a tall hat to hide her long rainbow hair.

'*Buongiorno!*' Marge smiles at me. 'That is how Italian people say hello!'

Jake and I start to giggle.

'He-ll-o,' Jakey replies in his robot voice. 'Buon-gior-no . . .'

'The rules are on the fridge,' Mummy tells Marge as she fishes in her handbag for the car keys. Looking at us, she adds: 'Remember to be polite and say "please" and "thank you" when Marge takes care of you.'

Daddy is heading towards the door. 'Be good, you two. Enjoy the party.'

'I won't know anyone there!' I gulp.

'Parties are a great opportunity to make friends,' Daddy says.

'Take a book to read,' Mummy offers, trying to be helpful.

I imagine myself sitting reading, away from everyone else playing and having fun at the party. It makes me feel sad.

Mummy and Daddy give Jake and I both a big kiss.

We stand on the doorstep waving them goodbye. As soon as the car disappears, Marge turns to me.

'Do you see this?' She shows me a tiny silver necklace with half a loveheart. I hold it in my fingers. There is small writing engraved on it. It reads: *Best Friends Forever*.

'This is a friendship necklace, given to me by Chester.'

'Who is Chester?' I ask.

Marge settles into Daddy's brown armchair and we come in close to listen to her story. Marge tells the best stories.

'I met Count Chester, the meerkat, at an amazing party. There were balloon elephants and fire jugglers and I somehow got stuck in a giant bubble! Count Chester used his tiny claws to poke a Marge-sized hole in the bubble and set me free.'

SIR PADDINGTON'S PARTY
"Set me free!!"

Jake and I are open-mouthed.

'We became best friends for life!' Marge smiles.

Marge slips off her jacket to reveal a black T-shirt with a lightning bolt across the middle and takes off her tall hat and out tumbles a mass of rainbow-coloured hair. Now she is really here!

'Let's read that list. Hop to it!' Marge twirls towards the fridge, her tiny shiny shoes tapping on the kitchen floor as she whirls. She reminds me of a coloured spinning wheel.

'Today I can only read upside down,' she announces, bending over as she reads:

1. Theo's present is in the top drawer
   – please wrap

2. Party is at 11 o'clock in Heath Park

3. Only one slice of cake at the party

Marge finds Mummy's fountain pen by the phone.

She crosses out 'only one slice' and writes NINE slices of cake.

'Yay!' yells Jake.

'Marge is in charge!'

'Let's not fill up on too much healthy food today. We need to leave plenty of room for cake!' Marge says, laughing. 'Let's get started,' she adds, so I show her the drawer with the present. It is a giant plastic water pistol!

'Ohh, let's open it now!' Marge suggests and Jakey grins and claps his hands.

'I don't think we should,' I warn them. 'Theo won't want a birthday present that's already been played with.'

Oh no! Marge is already breaking the rules. I feel knots in my belly – I don't want to get into trouble with Mummy.

But Marge is holding the box and looking really excited. 'At the palace we had an official toy tester whose job was to make sure all the toys work before they are given as gifts! Today we can be the toy testers!'

'Fantastico,' Jakey agrees, nodding. Jakey

only says 'Fantastico' whenever something truly amazing happens. Like the time he won a competition for eating the most strawberry shoelace candy.

I can't help but smile. Toy testers? I guess that makes sense. Marge has already succeeded in cheering me up.

Marge grins and adds a new rule to Mummy's list.

Have a water fight before the party

We open the box and fill up the water pistol. But we don't fill it with water – we fill it with apple juice, because Marge says then we can take a sip if we get thirsty. Marge puts on her sunglasses.

'I don't want juice in my eyes,' she explains. 'I have very sensitive eyes. At the palace, I used to polish the tiny emeralds and rubies on the Queen's crown because my eyes were able to see even the tiniest fleck of dust.'

When the apple-juice pistol is ready I want to take a turn first because I am the eldest, but Jakey grabs it from me.

'Hey,' I say, and I snatch it back and then Jakey gets mad and pulls my hair!

OUCH. It really hurts. Mummy normally puts Jakey on time out when he is naughty but she isn't here and my eyes begin to fill with tears.

'Jake!' Marge scolds, peering over the top of her sunglasses. 'If anyone used their arms and legs to get their own way at the palace, they were made to trim all the hedges in His Majesty's gardens with nail scissors!'

Jake looks surprised. 'Nail scissors are tiny. And hedges are huge!'

'Exactly,' says Marge. 'Please apologise.'

'I'm sorry, Jemima,' my little brother says quietly. And would you believe that he gives me a hug? I ruffle his blond hair affectionately. I can't help it – no matter what my brother does, I love him so much.

Then we have the most amazing juice-gun fight . . .

SPLISH! goes the juice on my dress!

SPLASH! goes the juice on Jake's jumper!

WOOF!

SPLOSH! goes the juice on Marge's smart black shoes!

We end up wrestling on the carpet and Archie starts chasing his tail and barking! I don't think I have ever laughed so hard in my life. Eventually Marge decides it's time to get ready, and we have to wash our hands and faces because of the apple juice.

Now my little brother has two rules (as well as no-broccoli-eating or hair-washing):

1. He won't wear a hat (even in the summer)

2. He never washes his face — EVER

But, would you believe it, when Marge asks him, he washes his face and even uses soap — **wow!**

He looks very pleased with himself as well.

Back in the living room, Marge notices the gold shiny wrapping paper for wrapping

Theo's birthday present.

'Ooh, that paper would
make lovely party hats,'
she says. 'Party hats are
incredibly useful. All good parties end in a
cake fight and party hats will protect our
hair!'

So we make hats and as we cut and glue
Marge tells us the best story ever. It is about
a spectacular cake fight that happened on her
last birthday. At the end of the fight, she was
covered in a twelve-tier pink sponge cake
with chocolate mousse icing.

'There was cake wedged in butler Jones's
reading glasses and I had chocolate mousse
up my nose and behind my ears for a week,
and all because we didn't have hats!'

I most definitely do not want cake up my
nose! I once got a frozen pea stuck up there

and Mummy made me blow my nose until it popped out. It really hurt.

Even though Mummy never lets Jakey use the grown-up scissors, Marge does, but she stands by his side the whole time. Jake cuts out three crowns from the shiny paper very carefully, with his tongue poked out in concentration, and I paste glitter, jewels and beads onto them.

Marge ties the hats on with string. We

look like three glorious kings as we parade around the whole house! I still can't believe that Jake has agreed to wear a hat. As we parade around, Marge sings us a song:

'Off we go now
Hear us sing
Wearing crowns
We'll visit the king!'

I dance around like a ballerina while Jake follows, banging a wooden spoon as loudly as he can on a saucepan. Marge tells us that the last time she was in a royal procession she was nine years old.

'I secretly untied the Grand Duke's boot laces as he marched across the drawbridge and he tripped over and landed in the moat!'

Jakey thinks this is hilarious.

I am curious. 'Was the Duke cross with you?'

'No! He had a lovely swim with the royal swans. Swans are very snuggly, you know, because of their long necks.'

I try to picture cuddling a swan and it makes me laugh again. I bet Marge was a very naughty child, like Jakey.

At last we come to rest in the living room.

'What will we wrap Theo's water pistol in now?' I ask.

Marge closes her eyes and says in a serious voice:

> '*Hocus pocus*
> *help me to focus!*'

Then she reaches into her bag and a long yellow silk scarf appears magically! She ties an enormous bow around Theo's present.

'Harry Houdini taught me how to tie a bow like that,' Marge says.

'Who's Harry Houdini?' Jake and I ask in unison.

'The world's greatest magician. He could disappear and reappear from anywhere.'

'Archie our puppy does that at the park!' says Jake.

We all look at Archie and decide that he must be a magical dog.

Marge tips her head upside down and consults Mummy's list again.

'It says to arrive at the party at eleven o'clock.'

Jakey and I look up at the clock. The big hand is on the six and the little hand is on the ten. I count on my fingers.

'Marge, that's in half an hour,' I say.

'No, that's in twenty hours,' Jake says, correcting me. Marge and I exchange a look. Jakey hasn't learned to tell the time yet but we don't want to embarrass him.

'Let's get dressed,' says Marge. 'All parties have a dress code. Usually something very bright and special for birthdays.' She leads us upstairs to our bedroom, two steps at a time. Our puppy Archie chases after us, and Marge

explains that the dressing-
up includes him too!

Archie's furry head is
cocked to one side. I think
he can understand English,
but no one except Jakey believes me.

'I don't think dogs are invited,' I say.

Marge is riffling through my closet but
pauses to protest. 'Dogs love parties and
birthday cake as much as people do, although
you must always brush their fangs with mint
toothpaste afterwards.

So we decide on my green lace dress for
Archie. It's too big, but I have to admit the
colour really suits him.

I put on my best dress. It's bright pink.
Jakey lets me dress him in the blazer he
got from Granny at Christmas. He even
manages to do both buttons up!

After we are dressed Marge
tells us that no party is complete
without a lot of balloons! Inside Marge's
magical bag is a large packet, all in different
colours. So we sit in a circle huffing and
puffing and blowing up as many
balloons as we can. I choose the
blue and red ones and Jake blows
up the yellow and green and Marge
blows up two at a time of any colour she can
find! After a few minutes her face is as red
as a tomato and Jakey is panting so
much that it's making me laugh.

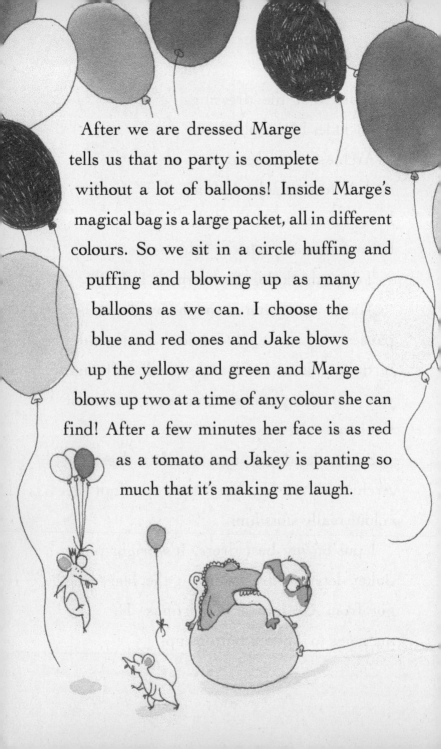

'Let's let them go,' says Marge, watching hers float up to the ceiling.

The balloons get bigger and bigger and we blow up more and more. Soon our living-room ceiling is hidden in rainbow bubbles. There are so many balloons I almost can't see Jakey or Marge!

'I once got my feet
tangled in fifty balloons
and floated all the way to Wimbledon,'
Marge declares, popping her head out
between the balloons. 'My hairdo was
completely ruined in the wind and everyone
saw my knickers! It was embarrassing.'

Jake grabs a purple balloon and sits on it
like a whoopee cushion. **POP!**

We all giggle.

'Marge . . .' I say, looking at the clock again,
'I think it's time to go!' I hate being late.

We leave the house with Archie dragging
his dress behind him and an enormous cloud
of rainbow balloons all bobbing and bumping
into each other above our heads! I start to
feel nervous again.

I have brought my book with me,
just in case I get bored or lonely.

Theo's party is under the big oak tree in the little park near our house. It has been decorated with streamers and a banner reading 'FIVE YEARS OLD TODAY'. There is a chequered tablecloth laid out over a wooden bench covered with cupcakes and sandwiches and a big pile of presents. Behind the bench is a giant bouncy castle.

Now if there is one thing Jakey and I really love in the world it is bouncy castles. I wish my whole bedroom was a bouncy castle and that the bottom of my tennis shoes were made of bouncy castle too!

All the little boys are very happy to see Jakey and they say hi to us. I notice a few of them have their big siblings with them too. Josh's big sister Posy is here and Lucy Walker as well. I feel much much better seeing other girls my age at the party. Everyone laughs when they see Archie in a dress, particularly Theo! Theo doesn't even mind when Archie manages to steal a peanut butter cupcake.

'Happy Birthday, Theo!'

Marge, Jakey and I chorus as we hand over his present. Theo looks surprised by the yellow bow.

'Don't worry,' Marge tells him, 'we tested the water pistol out for you. It's ready to use and full up with apple juice!'

'Thanks!' says Theo, taking in Marge's height. 'Are you a child or a grown-up?' he asks, which makes me giggle.

Jakey explains very politely that Marge is actually a small grown-up. But that she is tall enough to ride a bike without training wheels, which is the only thing that matters.

Just as we take off our shoes to go onto the bouncy castle, disaster strikes! The sky clouds over and it starts to rain. At first it's just the pitter-patter of little drops but soon they turn into big fat blobs of water. Theo looks like he might cry. I would be really disappointed too if it were my birthday.

Theo's mummy explains that we can't go onto the bouncy castle when it's wet as it's too slippery and slidey. 'We don't want anyone bumping heads,' she says.

But Marge has the most brilliant idea. 'Marge to the rescue!' she calls as she gathers all the balloons we brought with us.

She ties them into a vast bundle, so big and thick it makes a roof for the bouncy castle. No rain can get in at all!

All the parents clap and cheer. I feel so proud that we brought Marge to the party and that she is our babysitter.

'Everyone on the bouncy castle,' Theo's mummy shouts and we all scramble up excitedly. Even Archie scampers up with us.

BOUNCE!

SKIP!

His furry ears flap as he gets bounced up and down.

What fun! Whenever I am on a bouncy castle I imagine what it would be like to be a bird and be able to fly. Jakey is jumping so high his trousers keep slipping down!

JUMP!

HOP!

After a while our legs are tired and we sit down in the bouncy castle looking for something else to do. But it's still raining so we can't run around in the park yet. Theo's mummy and daddy are looking anxious – all the party plans are going wrong.

I am just about to ask everyone if they want me to read them a chapter from my book but then Marge jumps into the bouncy castle with another brilliant idea.

'By day I am Magnificent Marge, Masterful Babysitter of Jemima and Jakey Button. But by night I am . . . Magical Marge the Magician!'

What is Marge up to? I wonder. We all crowd around Marge to see.

'I need a drum roll,' she says dramatically. Theo's big sister Lucy is standing next to me and she claps her hands as loudly as she can.

I join in and soon everyone is clapping.

Marge twirls round and loses her balance on the grooves in the bouncy castle, her skinny legs buckling, but recovers quickly. Theo's little brother Matthew tries not to giggle.

Then Marge does a loud fake cough, covering her mouth with her hand, and when she pulls it away, there is . . . a purple silk handkerchief!

'Abra-ca-zebra!' she cries, looking very pleased with herself. 'Now, this looks like an ordinary handkerchief, but look again.'

We peer closely at the purple handkerchief. There is nothing weird about it, but then . . .

Marge's nose begins to twitch and she emits an enormous sneeze.

The birthday boy is unimpressed. Theo says, 'You don't need to be a magician to sneeze!'

But Marge smiles mysteriously and blows into the handkerchief as if it were a balloon. Then she shakes the purple silk and lo and behold, out fly twenty pink lollipops!

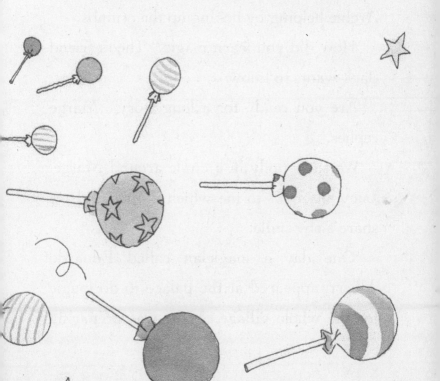

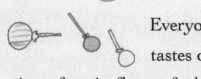

Everyone grabs one. Mine tastes of watermelon which is my favorite flavour for lollipops, even though I don't like the actual fruit.

Then Marge enlists the help of Archie as her magician's assistant! For her second trick she pulls a peanut butter cupcake out of her hat and then eats it using no hands, with Archie helping by licking up the crumbs.

'How did you learn magic?' Theo's friend Jack wants to know.

'Are you ready for a long story?' Marge replies.

We sit happily in a circle around Marge. Lucy sits next to me which is nice and we share a shy smile.

'One day a magician called Eduardo Alberti appeared at the palace to do magic for the whole village. As he was preparing for his grand show his assistant was trampled by a herd of pink flamingos. So he picked me and my twin sister Midge to be his assistants!'

Marge has a twin sister called Midge? I can't wait to meet her.

'What did you have to do?' asks Theo, his eyes as wide as saucers.

'Eduardo hid me in a box so you could only see my head and shoulders, and Midge in the other half of the box so you could only see her knees and legs – and then he sawed us in half!'

We all scream in unison.

'Show me how to do the tricks,' begs Theo.

'As a member of the Magic Triangle,' Marge says seriously, 'I am sworn to secrecy.'

Jakey and I can't believe it.

Marge has led the most incredible and amazing life of any grown-up we know!

Next up she juggles three balloons – well, she starts juggling with five, but one floats away and another pops when Archie bites it.

'Now for my final trick,' Marge says as she produces a deck of cards with a flourish. Suddenly she throws them into the air and sings:

'Cards, cards fly up in the air,
Make the weather fine and fair.
On this magical birthday,
Send the rain far away!'

We all scamper around catching the cards as they fall about us. I reach high to catch the ace of hearts.

'Look!' shouts Lucy.

We stare up at the sky. Would you believe that it has completely stopped raining?

I look at Jake's face. His eyes are bulging in disbelief. Is Marge a real magician?

We scramble out of the castle and back into our socks and shoes.

The boys all take off, stretching their little legs and hollering with joy.

But now there seems to be another problem. Theo's father takes a phone call, then switches off his phone.

He does not look happy.

'The face painter's car has broken down in a big puddle. He can't come.'

Marge doesn't need to be asked twice. 'Luckily . . .' she announces gallantly, 'I was taught face painting by one of the princess's ladies in waiting, and I am actually very good.'

She reaches into her bag and brings out some make-up and pens. We form a queue around the bouncy castle waiting for our turn.

I am a little hesitant to have Marge paint my face as she once tried to use Mummy's hair dye as a face mask!

She draws white make-up and pink lipstick on Lucy's face. 'You are Mary Antoinette, the French queen!' Then she paints my eyes with black eyeliner, which tickles at the beginning but then feels kind of nice, and my lips bright red. 'You are Cleopatra!'

Marge transforms Theo, Jakey, Peter, Matthew and Daniel into warlords and vikings and puts cat whiskers on herself, Zach and Stella, but Posy doesn't want her face painted so she just watches.

Marge really has saved the day.

Lucy and I wander away from the party and take turns on the swing. I show her my red tongue from the watermelon lollipop and she shows me hers and we giggle.

Can you believe it that Lucy also has a little brother like me, she has also lost five teeth like me and she also has a secret diary that not even her mummy knows about. We have so much in common!

It's time for the party games.

The first game is Pass the Parcel. My mummy always makes sure everyone gets a present when we play this game on mine or Jakey's birthday. But Marge doesn't seem to know the rules. When the parcel reaches her, she just passes it from her left hand to her right hand until the music stops.

'I win!' she laughs, unwrapping a layer of paper.

'Marge!' I scold her. 'You have to share the present!'

'Sorry!' says Marge guiltily. 'When I lived in the palace, the King always let me win!' She hands the parcel along and Theo's little brother Matthew finally wins!

After the games, Theo's mummy calls out: 'Everyone sit down, please!'

It's time to sing 'Happy Birthday' to Theo and eat cake, so we find a place to sit cross-legged in front of the picnic bench.

'Happy birthday to you, Happy birthday to you,'

we all sing. Jakey's voice is the loudest as he hugs his best friend Theo.

Looking at Theo's big chocolate cake with five candles on it, I feel very hungry.

I sometimes wish, when I see a big cake like that, that I could stick my whole face into it and gobble it all up. But I remember to sit nicely as I lick my lips and wait patiently.

Just as the cake is placed in front of Theo and he draws in a big gulp of air to blow out the candles, Marge pops her head up and blows them out first!

Oh no! I think.

Silence. Everyone stops singing Happy Birthday. No one has ever blown out the candles before except the birthday person. What bad manners!

Theo looks like he might be about to cry.

But suddenly the five candles re-light, and we all gasp.

Candles re-lighting by themselves?

'What happened?' asks Theo. He looks confused.

'It's because YOU are a secret magician,' Marge tells Theo.

'But I have never been a magician before,' Theo says.

'I made the wish for you,' Marge explains, 'when I blew out the candles. That's my birthday present for you. Candle wishes always come true.'

Theo gives a big puff and blows out the flames!

Whoopee!

Theo looks very happy, as though being a magician might be the best birthday present ever. Everyone claps and cheers and all the grown-ups take photos on their phones.

'How did you do that, Marge?' I whisper.

'It's just a trick!' Marge winks. 'A trick that I can't reveal unless you are a member of the Magic Square, which I am.'

'I think it's called the magic circle?' corrects Josh.

'Possibly,' concedes Marge.

Secretly I make a wish that Marge will always be our babysitter.

After this we all get stuck into the food and Marge says that the children are allowed nine slices of cake each, but after the sandwiches and crisps and fruit salad and sweets and nuts and popcorn I am too full to eat more than three slices of birthday cake and Jake only manages one (very big) one.

Marge reaches into her bag and pulls out her gold paper crown that we made earlier.

'So no one throws cake at me,' she whispers to Lucy and we laugh.

'I am going to nap before the cake fight starts,' Marge yawns. 'You know, Countess La Roo was able to marry off her two daughters by teaching them magic,' our babysitter warbles as she curls up with Archie. And there she lies, her feet poking out from behind the bouncy castle. Her gold crown is lopsided and her face paint is smeared. But she is sound asleep. Lucy and I decide she looks adorable.

'Shh,' says Lucy. 'She needs her sleep after all that work. How old do you think Marge is?'

'Jake thinks that she is one hundred and fifty-one,' I whisper and we head over to where the other kids are playing.

I have a fantastic time playing with Theo, Jakey and Lucy. We play Follow the Leader, with me and Lucy at the front and all the younger children following, until we arrive at the swings. Then Jake and Theo take turns pushing all of us back and forth.

HONK HONK!

I can hear Daddy's horn!

I look over and see Mummy and Daddy getting out of the car.

'*Buongiorno!*' I say as I run and give them a hug. They look exhausted from their long drive.

'How was the party?' asks Daddy.

'I made a new friend called Lucy,' I tell Mummy.

'That's great, Jemima! Well done,' says Mummy.

'It was the best party ever!' says Jakey.

We all thank Theo and his parents for a wonderful time and when Marge reappears with her hair tucked away and looking very sensible, they thank her for saving the day.

'I can't believe that Jakey wore a hat!' Daddy says when he hears about Jake's paper crown.

Then Mummy notices Archie.

'Is that your party dress, Jemima?' she asks me.

'Yes, Archie needed to be properly dressed to be a magician's assistant,' Marge explains.

Mummy and Daddy exchange a look.

'What a clever puppy putting it on all by himself. Amazing paw control!' Daddy jokes.

'He's the real Harry Houdini!' says Jake proudly and we all laugh and laugh.

Marge at Large
in School

Hi, Jemima Button here, with my little brother Jakeypants. There are lots of things that Jake and I don't agree on – like Jake prefers the shallow end of the pool and I like to swim in the deep end and I always eat sweets slowly to make them last and he gobbles them up in one go. But we both love to sit by the square window that looks down over our driveway. We call it the 'spying window'. Sometimes we spy on the neighbours walking their dog and sometimes we count how many green bins there are on our street, but right now we are waiting for someone.

Marge, our royal babysitter and favourite

grown-up (after Mummy and Daddy) is coming to take us to school today.

We are going to jump out and surprise her!

Even though it's seven o'clock on Monday morning and I have PE after lunch, I am still so excited because I love Marge. I love Marge as much as I hate PE (I'm the third slowest runner in our class).

As Marge's mint-green Mini Cooper screeches into the driveway, my heart is racing.

'In position!' Jake shouts.

We run downstairs and Jakeypants and I hide behind the front door. I have a sofa cushion as a weapon and he has a pillow. Our puppy Archie is with us as well and he keeps panting loudly.

'**Shhh,**' I tell him, 'or you'll have to hide somewhere else!

Marge can't know that we are here.' We wait, holding our breath. Her footsteps get closer. **DING DONG**, that's the doorbell!

Jake and I squeeze further back against the wall. The door handle turns.

Marge steps into the doorway. 'Hell-ooooo,' she calls to the empty hallway.

Jakey and I shout, **'ATTACK!'** and we both jump onto Marge.

I cling onto her back and Jakey throws his pillow first and then grabs her leg. Archie barks and wags his tail in excitement.

'Argh!' screams Marge in surprise as she flies forward onto the carpet. I wrestle her but she is so small and quick that she manages to roll away from us like a ninja.

'It's Marge the tickle monster,' she calls and begins tickling my chest and Jakey's feet. I throw a pillow at her head but she ducks.

We can't stop laughing and Archie is yapping at us all mangled in a heap.

'Kids, get off Marge right now, please.' Daddy sounds cross as he passes through the hallway into his office.

Jakey and I spring to our feet as Mummy appears in the hallway.

'Sorry, Marge!' Mummy apologises. She makes a stern 'we'll talk about this later' face at us.

But Marge is smiling as Mummy helps her to her feet. Marge is wearing a blue skirt with a beret, which is a kind of French hat that makes adults look silly.

'The list of things to remember is on the kitchen table,' Mummy says, grabbing Daddy's glasses for him, which he always forgets.

As Mummy gives Jake and me a quick kiss goodbye she says, 'Remember to be polite and say "please" and "thank you" when Marge takes care of you. And no more wrestling the babysitter!'

'Have you seen my glasses?' Daddy calls.

'I have them,' Mummy replies as they both head out the door.

'Bye, kids. Have fun at school,' our parents call as the door slams.

We run back upstairs and wave them goodbye from the spying window. When their car is as small as an ant Marge turns to us.

'*Bonjour*,' she sings as she pulls off her French beret and out tumbles her rainbow hair.

Holy hamburger!

It is plaited into a million tiny coloured braids with little bows on the end.

'*Bonjour* means hello in French. Now lets take a squiz at this list.'

I fetch the list and bring Mummy's fountain pen too as I know that Marge likes to add new rules of her own.

The list says:

1. Breakfast

2. Pack school lunches

3. Jakey must wear new school shoes

4. Drop off at school at 8 o'clock

'What's for breakfast?' Marge asks, swanning into the kitchen. 'I'm feeling a little peckish – what are you both making me? Hop to it!'

Jakey looks at me with one eyebrow raised. I giggle.

'Marge, you are the grown-up! YOU are supposed to be making breakfast for us!' I explain.

'Oh!' Marge is surprised. 'I've never made breakfast before. The Queen's cook Mabel used to bring me breakfast in bed every morning,' Marge says wistfully.

I am curious. 'What did Mabel make you?'

'Royal Pancakes,' Marge sniffs, 'with extra syrupy syrup.'

'I love pancakes,' Jake says. 'I'm hungry!'

My tummy is grumbling too. What are we going to do about breakfast?

'I am sure that I can make you a pancake,' Marge announces confidently. 'How hard can it be? If Mabel can do it, so can Marge!' She takes Mummy's pen and adds *Royal Pancakes* to the first rule. 'Marge's marvellous pancakes with extra syrupy syrup coming right up!'

Marge begins by rummaging around the kitchen in search of a pan and a bowl.

'You really don't have a butler or a chef to help me?' asks Marge after a while.

I giggle and shake my head. I wish we didn't have to go to school today. Spending time with Marge is so much fun!

I help Marge and together we mix some eggs and butter, flour and milk into a batter and Jake whisks it up. Then Marge turns on the stove.

'Back away, little servants,' Marge hollers as flames lick the giant pan. 'I don't want to burn down the kingdom!'

Jake and I step away as Marge pours the entire mixture into the pan.

'I am actually making crêpes which is French for pancakes. They taste even more delicious,' Marge exclaims.

'Don't you want to use the spatula thing that flips the pancakes?' I squint at Marge. 'That's what Mummy uses.'

'Nonsense. Mabel the royal cook never needed to rely on fancy utensils.
I am just going to toss it into
the air like ... THIS!'

Marge grabs the pan with both hands and tosses the pancake high into the air. Jake and I watch as it flies up, up, up and sticks **SPLAT** onto the ceiling!

'Call the guards, shut the drawbridge – we have a runaway pancake!' shouts Marge urgently.

I don't know what to think. The pancake is stuck on the ceiling and it doesn't look like it's going anywhere.

'I think we should call the fire department,' Jakey suggests. 'They have a big ladder that we can climb up to reach it.'

'That's silly,' I say. 'The fire department can only come for emergencies.'

'This is most definitely an emergency,' Marge says gravely.

We all stare at the pancake for a few moments, thinking. Then Marge suggests that we should just wait for it to drop back down into our mouths and catch it like Archie catches his ball.

But after we have waited for a while with our mouths wide open, my jaw is beginning to ache. 'I'm so hungry and tired,' complains Jake.

'Maybe it's still cooking,' Marge offers hopefully.

'On the ceiling?' I ask.

Just when we are close to giving up and getting some cereal instead, gravity gets the better of the pancake.

PLOP!

Down it falls and lands right in the middle of Marge's head!

'Breakfast is served! Tuck in,' Marge says.

We grab forks and Marge pours syrup all over her head and we eat it right off her hair in big gooey gulps! Jake is so hungry he ends up gobbling up half the pancake so I have to stop him before he eats any of Marge's multi-coloured hair!

'Here!' Jakey grabs Marge's beret. 'I think

you need to put your hat back on, your hair looks very sticky!'

Marge reads Rule Two aloud in a French accent: 'Pack school lunches.'

I show her where Mummy keeps our lunchboxes in the fridge. She looks suspiciously at the sandwiches, sniffing the bread and cheese. In the end she decides that they are delicious and healthy but that we must have treats too. So she fills the rest of our lunchbox with chocolate sprinkles from the baking drawer.

I grin and Jake claps his hands. 'Marge is in charge!' he declares.

Marge consults the list again. 'Now for Rule Three: Jake, Mummy says you have to wear your new school shoes.'

Jakey looks furious.

His little face has turned red like a traffic light. 'I hate wearing shoes!' he yells.

'All shoes?' asks Marge.

'Yes,' replies Jake. He looks determined.

So Marge runs out of the room and returns five minutes later with a big brown sack that she has collected from the hallway closet.

'Ta-da,' she says. 'It's Super Marge to the rescue!'

She turns the sack upside down and pours out a mountain of shoes. There are hiking boots, roller skates, clown shoes, flippers, stilts, skis and even a pair of ice skates!

'Do any of these look fun?' she asks my brother.

'I wanna wear the roller skates!' Jake says, grinning.

Marge laces them up.

'But I don't know how to roller skate!' confesses Jake.

'Don't worry,' Marge replies. 'They can teach you at school!'

'Let's bring your school shoes too, just in case,' I say sensibly, packing them in his rucksack.

'From what I've heard they can teach you everything at school,' Marge says. 'I would love to go myself one day.'

'Didn't you have to go to school when you were a kid?' I ask Marge.

Marge pauses to think for a moment, then curls into Daddy's armchair, which I am beginning to think of as Marge's story chair.

'Are you ready for a story?' Marge asks.

I love it when Marge tells us stories from her days at the palace. Marge gave up her life as a duchess because she hates rules. If you think living in a normal house has lots of rules, imagine living in a palace! But I don't want *too* long a story now because we have to go to school soon and I hate being late.

'Prince Rupert and I had a governess called Lady Morag. A governess is like a teacher for the royal family. She had pointy teeth and she made us practise piano until our fingertips were sore.'

PIANO CLASS:
With ~~Governess~~ Lady Morag
DRAGON

Oh no! Jakey and I share a look. She sounds terrifying. Poor Marge.

'One day Prince Rupert and I had had enough. We tricked Lady Morag into the dungeon and then locked her in with the rats and cobwebs.'

Jake claps his hands with glee, but I think the palace dungeon sounds scary. Marge seems to understand.

'We let her out again, of course,' she explains. 'It wasn't for long, but she learned her lesson. Lady Morag was much nicer to all the royal children after that!'

Marge stands up and we head to the door.

Suddenly Jakey's bottom lip starts to quiver and he bursts into tears. 'I don't want to go to school today!' he sniffs.

I know why my little brother is upset so I tell Marge. 'We are practising for the school concert first, before class.'

Jakey and I share music rehearsals with some of the other classes on Monday mornings. I like the practices but Jake says they are lame. He does not enjoy playing the recorder.

'It's BORING,' Jakey wails. 'I'm allergic to music.'

I give him a hug and try to cheer him up. 'You just have to practise the notes.'

Suddenly Marge springs to life and leaps onto the coffee table dramatically.

'By day, I am Magnificent Marge the Babysitter, but by night I am Marge the Musician.'

WOW! Marge is a musician too!

'I am the star of the Royal Brass Band,' Marge boasts.

'What's a brass band?' asks Jakey, his tears drying up.

'It's a group of musicians who all play brass instruments like trumpets, horns and the tuba,' explains Marge.

'Who is in the band with you?' I ask, imagining her princess friends.

'No one,' says Marge, 'I play all the instruments by myself. I like to promenade in the royal gardens wearing all of them around my neck.'

Jake seems to cheer up at this. 'Will you come to our school concert rehearsal?'

'Of course!' says Marge, gathering our schoolbags and putting her hat back on.

Phew, we are finally setting off for school!

It turns out roller skating is actually very hard! While Marge and I walk along the pavement chatting, Jakey's little legs pump faster and faster on the skates until we reach the top of a very big hill. After that he whizzes past us and disappears into some bushes! Extremely fast.

Marge and I look at each other, horrified. This reminds me of the time we lost Jakey at the supermarket when he was very small. He was finally discovered by Daddy lying under the shopping trolley, licking the wheels!

'Jakey?' I call, looking everywhere. I can't see him. My heart is starting to beat quicker. 'How will I tell Mummy that we lost Jakey?' I worry.

'He's not lost,' Marge explains. 'He's temporarily missing.'

We hear a scrabbling sound coming from the bushes. Then a brown squirrel darts out, followed by Jakey, who is covered in twigs and leaves. He grins from ear to ear. 'I love skating and I didn't even skin my knees!'

He's tired out, though, so I make him take the skates off and wear his school shoes. We are on our way to school again!

At the school gates our music teacher, Mrs Potts, is waiting to take the children to our music rehearsal. Marge introduces herself with an elaborate curtsy.

'How do you do? I was born Margery Beauregard Victoria Ponterfois and I . . . am a duchess.'

Mrs Potts seems quite surprised when Marge insists on attending the rehearsal, but after she points out that she is a musician herself in the Royal Brass Band, Mrs Potts allows her to come along.

I am slightly nervous about Marge being at school with us. What mischief will she create?

On the walk to the music hall I overhear Marge confiding in Mrs Potts, 'I've never been to a school before. My last governess taught me needlepoint and wild flower pressing!'

'You were home-schooled?' asks Mrs Potts.

'Palace-schooled,' corrects Marge.

Mrs Potts's mouth is open in surprise and Jakey and I can't help but stifle a giggle.

Everyone is staring at Marge as we enter the hall, as her beret hat is stuck on at a weird angle from all the syrup and she is doing an excited little jig on the spot.

Mrs Potts claps her hands twice for quiet and Jakey and I sit down with Rosie,

William, Lucy and Theo. They all remember
Marge from Theo's party and wave hello.
Marge stands at the front of the hall with our
music teacher.

'Good morning, girls and boys,' says Mrs
Potts. She smiles brightly as we all say good
morning back to her (except for Jakey, who is
looking nervously at the musical instruments
in the corner).

'Meet Jemima and Jake's babysitter, Margery Beauregard Victoria . . . *Porcupine*?'

Everyone laughs.

'Er, sorry if I got that wrong,' says Mrs Potts. 'Anyway, Marge is going to help us today.'

Marge takes a bow as if she is being given an award, then dances from foot to foot as if the ground is boiling hot, which makes everyone laugh.

Mrs Potts is looking flustered again.

'Oh no,' she says, rummaging through her papers. She turns to Marge. 'It appears I've left the sheet music behind. I'll be right back. Will you watch the children until I return?'

Marge nods enthusiastically.

Jake and I exchange a look. I can't believe that Marge is in charge of an entire hall of children!

As soon as Mrs Potts has left, Judy Briggs puts her hand up. 'Are you a child or a grown-up?' she asks Marge. Everyone giggles again.

'Jake will explain,' Marge replies.

So Jakey stands up and politely tells the whole class that Marge is actually a very small grown-up. But that she is tall enough to reach the middle shelf of the fridge, the cheese shelf, which is all that matters. Jakey loves cheese as much as I love sticker books. Everyone nods in agreement.

'Let's begin class,' Marge announces in an important voice. 'I am your temporary governess so please line up while I hand out your musical instruments.'

Marge has found the big blue bucket in the corner filled with all the instruments and is standing by it proudly.

As we make a line in front of Marge I notice that some of the boys are taller then Marge, which makes me giggle.

Marge closes her eyes and fishes into the bucket as if it were a lucky dip.

There is a beat of silence before she says, '*Voilà!*' and pulls out a clarinet.

She hands it to Rosie Williams, who looks confused.

'But I play the violin,' Rosie says as the rest of the class laughs.

Marge thinks for a minute. 'Not today you don't. Everyone should learn how to play as many instruments as they want. How else will you find the ones you like the most? I myself have fourteen favourite instruments.

I am as accomplished on the French horn as I am on the Scottish bagpipes.'

Marge fishes back into the bucket.

'Next!' she calls.

Judy is next in the queue and is given a guitar instead of her flute, then it's Jakey's turn.

Marge fishes into the bucket, humming with her eyes closed, and pulls out a triangle.

'But I don't know how to play it!' Jakey worries. 'And if I am not very good on the recorder I will be terrible on the triangle.'

'Nonsense,' says Marge. 'Just listen to your heart and you will make wonderful music. NEXT!'

I am the next in the queue and Marge fishes out a trumpet. I love the sound that a trumpet makes but I have never thought to play it before because I usually play the violin, and no other girls in my year play the trumpet.

Suddenly I feel quite excited to play a new instrument and I put my mouth around the end and blow –
PFF! A strange raspy sound comes out.

One by one all the instruments get handed out until nearly everyone has an instrument that they have never played before. There is a small tug-of-war over the drums that is quickly resolved by Marge deciding that all three boys can play them at the same time.

A handful of the younger children haven't lined up for an instrument.

'We don't want to play anything,' Mary Cooper complains. 'It's not fun.'

'I'm going to make a special instrument just for you!' Marge says cheerfully.

Marge busies herself in the corner. She fills an empty jam jar with paperclips, pins and staples and makes a colourful shaker.

'Ohh . . .' Mary looks thrilled as she makes a rattle sound with it.

So we all help to make instruments for other children without them. I find an empty coffee can and make a drum. Judy manages to make a rain stick for Harrison's little brother. Marge finds some old bells, ties them to pieces of ribbon and hands them out. Soon everyone is happy.

'Now we are ready for a concert!' cries Marge.

We're a little bit nervous, but gradually everyone starts playing.

'Close your eyes and make lots of noise! There is no wrong way to play music,' Marge says as she sways in front of us.

We are all blowing, banging, strumming, dancing, clapping and singing! The sound is so noisy that I can't hear my own trumpet even though it is very loud.

I look over at Jake. He looks so happy as he dings the shiny metal triangle in time to the music.

'You all sound brilliant!' Marge says enthusiastically. 'Let's share our wonderful music with the rest of the school!'

Marge flings open the door and leads the entire classroom along the corridor and out into the playground.

Even though it sounds terrible we are all having so much fun. I now understand why music makes you feel happy, even though I can't make anything but a raspberry sound come out of this trumpet. Rosie is playing her clarinet like it's a guitar and Lucy is wearing a drum on her head.

'It's my drum hat,' she says and bangs it. It makes the funniest sound!

Theo is playing the violin backwards! But you won't believe this – he's actually making a good noise. Jake is tinging his triangle proudly in time to the music and Marge is singing like she is in an opera! Her voice is shaky and shrill like a lost goat on a mountain top.

We end up in the centre of the playground and we are making such a racket that all the other kids and teachers come out of their rooms and form an audience.

At first no one knows what to make of us but soon the other kids start tapping their feet and clapping along and the teachers find it impossible to disapprove as we are clearly having so much fun. Even Mrs Turnball, our strict science teacher, is nodding her head in

time with the music, and some of the older kids are dancing!

My cheeks are hurting from blowing and laughing and everyone seems to love our crazy show!

I can't see Marge anywhere. Where is she?

Then I hear a deep sound and turn round. Marge is wearing Jakey's roller skates and has strapped a tuba to her neck. The tuba is like a trumpet for a giant and it is twice the size of her body! I have only seen an older girl called Martha play it once before.

Marge is blowing the tuba loudly and skating around us all.

Oh no, Marge, you have gone too far, I think. She is twirling way too fast as she sails past me.

Mr Lindon, our PE teacher, shouts, 'Watch out!' as Marge whizzes past him. But he is too late.

CRASH!
BANG!
SPLASH!

Marge has lost her balance and fallen face down into the little water fountain in the middle of the playground.

Zwiiiip!

We all can't stop giggling as Mrs Potts arrives back to see Marge upside down in the fountain with her head stuck inside the tuba and just her little legs poking out!

Everyone is laughing their heads off, but Jakey and I rush forward and help Marge out of the water. Jake and Theo take hold of the tuba and I grab her little feet, and try

to pull her out of it. Then Rosie takes a hold of me and helps pull, and Lucy takes a hold of Rosie, and Jamie and Peter take a hold of Lucy, and before I know it all the pupils have lined up and are pulling like a tug of war to get Marge free from the tuba. Until . . .

POP!

Marge is free! We all fall down but no one is hurt and I'm relieved that Marge is okay, even if the tuba is a little wet.

'Well done, my fellow musicians!' Marge praises us, and we end up in a big group hug.

Just then Mr Siles, our headmaster, appears in the playground. 'All right, everyone, back to class,' he says sternly. He raises an eyebrow at the sight of Marge, soaking wet, in a beret, holding a tuba.

'Marge, it's time for lessons now,' I explain.

'Can I join your class?' she replies, running ahead to the classroom.

We all head back inside and the morning passes quickly. I can tell that everyone is in a good mood after our concert in the playground. Even Mrs Potts doesn't seem to mind about the tuba and in Maths Mr Bates gives us prizes for getting our answers right! I get the 'Star of the Day' certificate and Marge wins three gold stickers.

At breaktime Marge gives Jake, Theo, Jamie and Peter roller-skating lessons in the playground. Then in PE Marge convinces Mr Lindon that all throwing and catching should be done to music. It turns out that I never miss the ball when I am listening to Marge singing loudly, and for once I really enjoy PE!

In Art Marge suggests that we should finish our self-portraits blindfolded. I thought our art teacher, Mr Brock, was going to lose his temper when Ella painted on Drew's sweater by accident and James knocked over an entire pot of green paint . . . but by the end of class even Mr Brock agreed that everyone's portraits looked more unusual and that the exercise had 'unlocked our creativity'. It's so much fun having Marge at school!

BING! Now it's time for lunch.

We tidy up the art room and fetch our lunchboxes, ready to sit in our lunch circle. As I'm walking back to our classroom, Jakey pops up beside me. 'Mrs Potts said that I can join your class for lunch today because I was so well-behaved in music rehearsals.'

I can tell that Jakey is excited to see our babysitter again, and when we walk through the door we see that Marge is sitting in the middle of the floor. Jakey runs to give her a hug. Our form teacher, Mr Gale, looks a little surprised, but I don't think he minds.

'Could you look after the children while I eat my lunch in the staffroom?' he asks Marge.

'Of course!' Marge agrees, giving Jakey a big smile.

As we sit down in a circle around her, Marge brings out a lunchbox and a giant spoon from her handbag.

'In the palace we had an official food tester whose job was to make sure that no one poisoned the King or Queen!' She grins hopefully at us.

Everyone is happy to share a bite of their lunch with Marge.

One spoonful of Jack's jam sandwich . . .

YUM!

Two spoonfuls of Sarah's pasta . . .

TOO COLD!

Half of Rosie's peanut butter and apple . . .

TASTY!

ALL of Eli's fish fingers . . . **DELISH!**

Marge rubs her belly and sighs. 'In the palace, after lunch we always had nap time. A duchess can get very tired, you know.'

Marge stretches and snuggles into the beanbag in our library corner, next to her tuba.

'Will you read me a book?' she asks in a baby voice.

Lucy and I run and get our favourite storybook and Eli gets a blanket from the cupboard. When Marge is tucked up, we read her a bedtime story. Jakey is in charge of turning the pages and everyone joins in. We pass the book around the class and take it in turns to read a page each.

Once we have finished the story Marge's eyes are closing.

'Can you leave the light on?' Marge asks. 'I'm scared of ghosts.'

Jakey rolls his eyes. 'There is no such thing as ghosts! Even I know that and I'm only four.' He really is brilliant at eye rolling.

'Yes there are,' Marge replies. She pulls her blanket off and covers her head with it.

'Whoooo!' she calls in a ghostly voice.
'Whooo ...'

Everyone in the class starts to giggle. Marge is so funny.

'It's me, Marge the magnificent ghost!' she jokes.

Then Marge yawns sleepily, cuddles up to the tuba and promptly dozes off.

When he gets back from lunch Mr Gale is very impressed at how quietly we're sitting in our lunch circle. He doesn't seem to notice that Marge is asleep in the corner and we are only being quiet because we don't want to wake her up.

I can't stop thinking about Marge for the rest of the day. I go from class to class wondering if Marge is still asleep or if she is up to any more mischief. I wish I could peek in on her and see if she is still asleep on the beanbag but I don't have time and the day seems to whizz past.

BING!

That's the bell telling me that school is finished for the day!

At the school gates I find Mummy, Daddy and Jakey waiting for me.

'How was school, Jemima?' Daddy asks.

'I played the trumpet today!' I brag. 'And I didn't miss the ball once during throw and catch in PE.'

'How were music rehearsals for you, Jakey?' Mummy asks my little brother. She looks a little worried because he usually complains all the way home from school on Mondays.

'I LOVED music rehearsals,' Jakey says happily. 'Marge taught me to play the triangle and Mrs Potts said that because I like to play it so much I can play it again next week!'

'Marge was in school?' Mummy asks, surprised.

At that moment I hear a familiar sound and we all turn to look.

Marge is walking out of the school with the tuba around her neck playing a very loud tune. She gives us a big smile.

'I blew all the water out of it!' Marge announces. 'Mrs Potts says that I can join the school band too. I just need to practise a bit at home first,' Marge says excitedly.

Mummy and Daddy share a look as Jakey and I crack up laughing.

'Where's my horse and carriage to take us home?' Marge asks innocently.

'Very funny, Marge,' Daddy replies, pointing to our old blue car. Then he flings open the back door, bows down very low and cries, 'Your carriage awaits, Your Royal Highness!'

I'm giggling because Marge seems to bring out the funny side in everyone.

'*Merci!*' replies Marge in a posh voice. 'That is French for thank you,' she explains as we all bundle inside.

I can't help smiling all the way home as

Jake and I cuddle up with Marge on the back seat and Mum and Dad ask us questions about our day.

Who would have thought that our babysitter would need picking up from school too? Marge definitely isn't an ordinary grown-up, but to me she's the best babysitter in the whole wide world.

Marge the
Pirate Nanny

Hello again – it's me, Jemima Button. I'm back. I am so excited for today because Marge our extraordinary babysitter is coming over. We used to be an ordinary family until she came along. I know what you are thinking – babysitters are boring – but you haven't met Marge. Incredible things happen whenever Marge is around. Like the time she led our entire school in an outdoor concert with her head stuck in a tuba. Or when she wanted to tie balloons to Jakey's feet to see if he would float to school.

The only bad part is that our cousin, baby Zara, is also going to be here.

I am trying to keep my mind off that by drawing a self-portrait (which is a picture of myself) to show Marge. I am the second best drawer in my class after Emily Fox, who can draw fingers and toes perfectly.

Jakeypants is still my little brother, even though sometimes I wish he wasn't. And he still loves wrestling and dinosaurs, but now he also loves pirates. At the moment he's sitting next to me on a blanket in the garden, building a pirate ship out of Lego.

We haven't seen Zara for a while (thank goodness) and apparently now she can crawl. When she was born she was a bald blob with eyelashes and she couldn't do much at all. Mummy says I looked just the same when I was small, and that we could be 'sisters'! But we are definitely not sisters because Zara is very naughty.

No one believes Jakey and me when we say that Zara may look like an angel but she is definitely not one. I have written in my secret diary a list of all the bad things that she has done to me:

1. DRAWING all over my library book

2. SQUEEZING toothpaste into my dolls' house

3. PULLING the head off my Beach Barbie

Would you believe
that I couldn't find
my Barbie's head
anywhere? Then
the next time Daddy
turned the oven on
there was a horrible
smell and out came a hairy yellow alien.

Still, I lined up all my dollies in a row
by the front door to welcome Zara today.
Except for Sarah, my Cabbage Patch doll.
I cut Sarah's hair short and now she looks
a bit scary. I don't want her to frighten my
little cousin because when Zara cries it is
so loud I have to put my fingers in my ears.
Last time we saw her, Daddy nicknamed
her 'the ambulance' because when she got
upset she sounded like a siren:

WAA-OOH, WAA-OOH!

'That bad baby is NOT allowed to go near my toys,' warns Jake. 'Especially Pete.'

Pete is the soft-toy dinosaur my brother has slept with every night since he was born. My little brother has two rules:

1. Nobody is allowed to touch Pete, EVER

2. He won't step foot in any sandpit as he's scared of being stuck in 'quicksand'

This morning he copied me and lined up Pete and two trucks to welcome Zara. Except that he also built a barrier of books so she can look but not touch.

Jakey will not forgive Zara. When we met her for the first time, Mummy let him cuddle her. He was very gentle and even sang her a song . . . but she vomited green stuff all over his new white shoes.

YUCK.

And then – would you believe it? – she laughed.

But that's not the only reason Jakey hasn't forgiven Zara. Last time she came to our house, as soon as Mummy left the room, she unscrewed the lid of her cup and tipped orange juice over his head. Then, while he was wiping his face, Zara pulled down his trousers!

My aunt claimed it was an accident, but Jakey and I know it wasn't.

Who knows what trouble that baby will get into today, now that she can crawl? At least we will have Marge to protect us.

DING DONG

Archie, our pug-nosed puppy, is barking. I can hear Mummy's heels *click-clack* on the wooden floor as she hurries to let them in.

I peer through the French doors. There in the hallway is my Auntie Sally with the pink pram. Zara's pram. I can already feel my heart start to beat a little faster.

The back door swings open as Mummy and Sally push the pram outside, chatting happily. Its big wheels are chopping through the grass. I spy one of Zara's small chubby hands waving. There is no escape now.

Archie lowers his head and covers his eyes with his paws. I wish I could make a run for it, but I need to be a big girl today if I want to spend time with Marge and show her my drawings.

The pram's wheels grind to a halt.

'What a good baby-waby you are!' gushes Sally as she scoops her daughter out of the pram.

Our little cousin does look sweet. She has dark curly hair and today it is held back with a giant purple bow.

Jake obviously doesn't think she looks sweet though. 'With those fat thighs she could be a sumo wrestler,' he tells me. Although he whispers this in my ear, it's like Zara has heard him.

'**Ga-ga**,' she says, and points her tiny finger at me.

A shiver wriggles down my spine.

'Ga-ga?' I raise an eyebrow at Jake.

'"Ga-ga" means "I am going to get you",' Jakey whispers.

We share a nervous giggle as Zara stares daggers at us. Hopefully Marge will know how to make sure she behaves herself.

I give our auntie a big hug, careful not to squash the baby, and she tells me that I look taller. Jakey shows Sally his front tooth which is becoming wobbly. She seems impressed.

As Sally gives Zara to Mummy, Mummy starts speaking in a baby voice.

'Hello, Zara, ba-ba boo-boo, baaa.'

Zara looks confused.

Why do grown-ups always talk to babies like they are stupid?

Mummy squeezes Zara's cheeks and she chuckles, acting cute.

'Marge should be here shortly,' Mummy promises Sally.

They are going out for a special dinner to celebrate Sally's birthday. With Daddy away working, Marge is in charge of us.

DING DONG

That's the doorbell again!

'I'll get it!' Jakey bolts past me. His shorts are already over his head like a wrestling mask and he is making his aeroplane-taking-off sound.

THUD – now he's tripped over.

'Oww!' he shouts, annoyed. His face is redder than a fire engine.

I think he is about to say something else when Mummy reminds him, 'No rude words.' She gives him a cuddle and he dashes inside the house.

Jakey has had a potty mouth lately. Mummy got cross when he said a naughty word in front of his teacher last week, so now we have a chart on the fridge. We get one point if we use a bad word and Jakey has three points already. If he gets five, he isn't allowed to use his bike all weekend.

The door opens and finally . . .

Marge is here!

She is wearing a plastic coat and hat and twirling an umbrella. 'I know it's not raining but babies can be messy, so I came prepared!' Marge's smile is as big as a slice of watermelon.

Jakey scampers underneath her coat. 'I hate babies!' he says, hiding.

'Me too.' Marge winks as she bends down to Jakey's height, which isn't very far for her even though he is only four years old.

'Do you know who LOVES babies more than anyone?' she asks us.

'Mummy?' I guess.

Marge shakes her head.

'Who then?' Jakey blinks.

'. . . Pirates!' she whispers.

Our eyes widen in shock. Marge is full of surprises.

'Here,' I say, holding out my picture shyly. 'I drew a self-portrait.'

Marge stares at it for a long time. 'You are a wonderful artist, Jemima. If the Queen saw this, she would frame it for all to see.'

My heart is bursting with pride! I can't

wait to show Marge the rest of my drawings. Marge is actually a duchess, which means she is related to the royal family. It also means that she sometimes expects a carriage to pick us up or a butler to fetch our dinner.

Just then Mummy and Auntie Sally appear to say hello. I can tell that Sally is shocked by how small Marge is. Did I tell you that our babysitter is only the size of about seven packets of biscuits stacked on top of each other?

'Looking after Zara is easy breezy,' my aunt brags.

Zara may be acting cute now but Jakey and I exchange a look – we know differently.

There's lots of chatter as Mummy, Marge and Sally have a cup of tea and talk through the list of rules for looking after the baby. Then Mummy puts the list on the fridge. Sally makes sure that Zara is snuggled happily asleep in Marge's arms before she whispers goodbye and tiptoes towards the door.

'And remember,' Mummy tells us quietly, 'be on your best behaviour and help Marge with your baby cousin while we're out.' She kisses us both and waits for us to promise.

'I will,' I smile.

But is Zara going to be on *her* best behaviour?

'I won't,' Jakey scowls. 'The only babies I like are baby T. rexes!'

Sally and Mummy laugh, but I am a bit worried.

'If there are any rude words, put a point on the chart, please,' Mummy tells Marge.

Marge nods as she gently puts the baby into her pram.

Zara's eyes are shut, but one hand is gripped in a fist. Is she really asleep?

We all traipse outside and I wave goodbye to Mummy as they drive away.

'Goodbye, kids, and remember – Marge is in charge!'

The minute our old blue car disappears, I turn back to the house. Jakey is playing sumo wrestlers with Marge on the grass so I go over to check on the baby. I tiptoe very quietly and as I peer inside the pram I can see . . . it's empty. My palms start to sweat. I knew that she was only pretending to be asleep.

I glimpse a tiny foot disappearing around the corner of the house – Zara is heading for the back garden.

'Runaway baby!' I cry, racing after her.

Marge and Jakey follow at top speed.

In the back garden, Zara has discovered Jakey's Legopirate ship.

As we sprint towards her, I notice a wicked glint in her eye. Then she lifts the ship into the air as if it's a ball to throw . . .

Quickly our babysitter grabs her and passes me the pirate ship.

'Watch out, little scallywag,' Marge scolds. 'Or you will have to walk the plank!'

Zara gurgles crossly and Marge settles her back into the pram with a dummy.

'You see, babies are unpredictable. The only people they respect are pirates,' she says.

'Pirates?' I ask. I can't picture it.

'Yes,' Marge replies, sitting down on our blanket. She pulls Jakey onto her lap and I scooch in next to her.

I love it when Marge tells us a story.

'So . . .' Marge begins as she takes off her hat and out pours her rainbow hair glimmering in the sunshine.

I don't remember if I told you this, but our babysitter has red, green, yellow, orange and blue hair! The first time I saw it I couldn't believe my eyes! I'm not sure if Mummy and Daddy would let our royal babysitter look after us if they saw her crazy magical hair. But she only ever takes it out when we are alone with her.

'After I left the palace, I decided to sail to Africa on my ship, *Admiral Marge the Eighth*. I wanted to explore faraway lands and find a cure for my albino water buffalo's insomnia.'

'What's insomnia?' Jake asks.

'It's the opposite of *out*somnia, which is when you sleep all the time,' Marge explains. 'But halfway across the ocean, my ship was attacked . . . by pirates!'

I feel nervous suddenly. Jake's bottom lip is quivering, and even Zara looks scared.

'Their ship was called *The Poison Curse* and the captain was Not-So-Jolly Roger. But he was really rather soft and sweet inside.'

Captain Not-So-Jolly Roger

'He was?' Jakey gulps.

'Yes! He needed a nanny for the babies on board. So I took the job and Wesley, my albino water buffalo, befriended the captain's parrot, Pollyanna. The only thing that pirates adore more than treasure is babies.'

I don't know whether to believe Marge. I can't imagine a pirate captain cuddling a baby, no matter how soft and sweet he is!

Jake isn't sure either. 'Are there really babies living at sea?' he asks.

'Hundreds of them. When you think about it,' Marge reasons, 'babies and pirates have a lot in common.'

'They do?' we chorus.

'Of course! They both love shiny things. They take other people's stuff without asking, and they drink from bottles all day! All babies are pirates at heart.'

Jakey and I turn to each other. It does make perfect sense.

'Now let's read the list of rules,' Marge says, fetching it from the fridge door and coming back outside to hand it to me. 'Hop to it!'

'**GOOGA!**' Zara cries, snatching the list from me and biting a chunk out of the middle.

She chews twice, then spits it out.

YUCK, it's all soggy and I can't read it now.

But Marge isn't worried. 'I knew a pirate baby who chewed a whole treasure map once.' Her eyes twinkle with the memory. 'We don't need the list anyway. I've looked after a lot of babies at sea. We'll follow Marge's Pirate Code instead.'

196

I don't know how my aunt will feel about this, but Marge is in charge.

Rule 1. Zara needs a bottle of milk, not rum. She's not allowed rum until she is a fully grown pirate

Rule 2. Pirate babies need games to entertain them, treasure to play with and lots of cuddles

'Pirates love to snuggle babies,' Marge explains. 'When your job is being scary at sea all day long there is nothing more soothing than singing sweet lullabies at night.'

Jake looks at Zara and I can see his face soften. He moves over to the pram to give her a cuddle, but my baby cousin has other ideas.

YANK! Zara grabs Jakey's hair and tugs.

'STUPID SHORT-LEGS!' Jakey
hollers.

Uh-oh, that was rude of him. Mummy
would not like that one bit.

But Marge continues with her Pirate Code.

Rule 3. No rude words, unless we are in battle at sea, or your parrot poops on your shoulder

She winks at me. 'Are we all on board, me
hearties?'

We both nod. I can tell Jake is imagining
himself in a dangerous battle at sea. Marge
won't have to put a point on the chart if Jake
sticks to the code.

'Then you're ready for your pirate names!'

Rule 4. All shipmates need a pirate name

Jakey sticks his tongue out at Zara.

'Her name can be Captain Fat Thighs!'

Zara does NOT look pleased with that name. She is beginning to look upset.

'Or Blackbeard?' suggests Marge to cheer her up.

But it doesn't work. Zara's face is now the colour of a ripe tomato.

'What about Captain Purple Bow?' I offer.

But it is too late. Zara starts to sob.

The sound of an ambulance siren begins.

WAAAAH-OOOOOH!

Marge takes Archie's paws and tries a silly dance to cheer her up but it isn't working.

WAAH-OOH! WAAAH-OOH!

Then I remember Marge's Pirate Code –
Zara must want a bottle!

I reach for one in her nappy bag.

Zara stops crying when she sees it.

Marge pats my shoulder in relief.

Zara takes the bottle
from me and then . . .

WHEEEEEE

With a toothy grin, she THROWS it.

We all duck our heads as it flies across
the garden, whizzes through the open
door and rolls into our house.

Is our cousin a superbaby?

Jakey looks impressed, like the time
I accidentally exploded our homemade
volcano on Daddy's work papers.

'Pirate babies love to throw things,' Marge says. 'Part of my job as a pirate nanny was collecting all the treasure that was tossed around the ship! The other part was only allowing babies to play with the *blunt* cutlasses. A cutlass is a real sword and very dangerous,' she explains.

'WAAH-OOH!' Zara is crying again. She has climbed out of her pram, crawled inside the house and is pointing under the sofa. Her bottle is trapped beneath it.

Jakey looks worried. 'Daddy says the sofa is too heavy to move. That's why he couldn't get my silver whistle.'

I bet it's not impossible to move the sofa. I know for a fact that Daddy had had enough of Jakey screeching on that whistle all the time.

We poke our heads under the sofa and Jakey tries using his tennis racket but it doesn't reach the bottle. I am doing my best to blow it out like the wolf from the three little pigs, but my lungs aren't strong enough.

Marge plops Zara on Daddy's chair and hitches up her skirt, revealing legs as skinny as toothpicks.

'Shiver me timbers!' she says determinedly, and using the hook end of her umbrella she manages to scoop the bottle out.

We high-five our pirate nanny and then look back at Zara.

Uh-oh. Zara is GONE!

Wasn't she on Daddy's chair just a moment ago?

'Pirate babies also love to play hide-and-seek,' Marge tells us. 'Once I found fifteen babies hiding in a pile of cannon balls!'

Sally and Mummy will not be happy if we can't find our little cousin.

We hunt around the living room . . . no Zara.

We search Daddy's office . . . no Zara.

We look in the kitchen and behind the curtains . . . no Zara.

I am starting to panic.

And what are these patches of water on the carpet?

There is a trail leading from the room like the ones our pet snails Bill and Bob leave, but much bigger.

'She must be teething,' Marge explains. 'When babies have teeth coming through they dribble a lot.'

Eww . . .

'FOLLOW THAT DROOL!' cries Jakey.

We follow the trail of little puddles along the hallway. The largest one is just outside the coat closet.

Marge's hands are on her hips. 'The trail ends here.'

Phew, we have found her!

'Gotcha!' Jakey opens the door and we discover Zara hiding in the coats, hugging my wellington boot.

I wave her bottle. Is she hungry?

But she grins cheekily and skedaddles down the hall. Jakey lunges for her, but she darts between his legs. This pirate baby is faster than a squirrel sneaking a nut. Marge dives to tackle her, but naughty Zara sinks her teeth into Marge's outstretched finger.

'Argh! I shall never play the harp again!' Marge gasps in pain.

We watch in shock as my baby cousin wiggles and giggles through the living room. Her purple bow flies behind her like a small cape.

TUG, she pulls all the magazines off the coffee table.

SMASH, she throws the TV remote across the room.

RIIIP, she tears Daddy's newspaper in half.

'Capture that sea robber!' Jakey orders, jumping onto the sofa and waving his tennis racket like it's a sword.

'Capture me a plaster!' Marge moans, holding out her bitten finger.

Zara is now quickly crawling up the stairs. I try to grab her leg but she squirms free, slipping around the banister and into our bedroom. I am panting as I reach the doorway.

'Don't knock over my . . .'

Before I can finish the sentence, disaster strikes. The castle that I have built out of magnet tiles and filled with princess figurines has been smashed over. It took me HOURS to build it! I am so mad I could scream.

Zara turns to me with a smirk.

'Ahoy, me matey!' Marge snatches Zara into her arms.

Jake is now inside our room too and shaking his head in wonder.

'That pirate baby is very bad AND very fast,' he says, taking in my broken castle. But he doesn't say a single rude word.

I am not having a fun time any more. Zara is ruining our day with Marge. Not to mention the mess she has made that I will have to clean up. Jakey hates tidying and always comes up with excuses for why he can't do it. Like the time he was 'temporarily blind' from watching too much TV.

I stomp downstairs with my arms crossed.

'I am going to scoot in the driveway,' I huff.

'Wait, Jemima. Please will you feed the baby? Young buccaneers are the best at bottle duty,' calls Marge.

Zara turns to me with big pleading eyes.

I sulk over and sit on the sofa with my baby cousin.

She nestles into my arms and looks up at me as she drinks from her bottle. I open the jar of apple sauce too, in case she wants that after her milk.

I find myself stroking her hair. It feels soft. She is so peaceful and gentle that I am not grumpy any more.

Just as I am thinking happy, loving thoughts, Zara tips the apple sauce all over my head!

It's dripping down my hair and into my eyebrows. I am covered in baby food. I taste it.

'Scrumdiddleyumptious!'

I say, trying to lick my own face like a cat.

I pass Zara back to Marge and wipe my face. At least now Zara is yawning and rubbing her eyes. She must need a nap. So Jakey and I help by fetching a blanket and closing the curtains. Once we have grabbed a snack from the kitchen, we take our scooters outside so Marge and Zara can have some peace and quiet.

After six races (I win two) and a cheese sandwich each, we are bored and creep back inside.

Oh NO!

There, curled up asleep in the pram, sucking on a dummy, is MARGE!

Wide awake and sitting cross-legged on the sofa is . . . baby ZARA.

I can't believe that our grown-up babysitter has fallen asleep inside a baby's pram. It's one thing being the same height as a child but quite another stealing their bed.

'Wake up!' Jakey prises open one of Marge's eyes.

Marge's chest is rising and falling as she snores.

I pull the dummy out of her mouth. Marge stirs slightly but still doesn't wake up.

POP!

Now I get the giggles and Jakey keels over laughing, but it's only when Zara shrieks with delight that Marge opens a sleepy eye.

'Can I nap for another three hours?' she asks, yawning.

'No,' I giggle.

'That tiny bed on wheels is so comfortable. I must get one for Wesley. It would surely cure his insomnia.' Marge stretches and tries to get out of the pram but her bottom is stuck.

We are laughing so hard our sides ache.

'Attention, pirates! Get ready to scrub the decks and let's finish the Pirate Code. **Heave-ho!**'

Marge's voice sounds strict but we can't take her seriously because she has moved into a squatting position to try to wiggle free. She looks so silly.

Jakey and I salute. 'Aye-aye, Captain Marge the Sleepy!'

Even Archie joins in, sitting in a line with us. He holds up his paw to our captain, Marge the Pirate Nanny.

And for the first time that day, Zara gives us all a sparkling happy smile, bubbling up with joy.

Finally Marge frees herself from the pram and gives us our pirate names. We write them on name-tags and stick them to our clothes.

Jakey is **Jakeypants the Fierce.**

Marge becomes **Marge the Pirate Nanny** (also known as **Marge the Sleepy**).

Archie looks surprised to be called **Salty Sea Doggy.**

Zara drools onto her new name, **Captain No Beard.**

And my pirate name is **Long John Jemima**!

The next part of Marge's Pirate Code is:
Rule 5. All shipmates must dress as pirates

I am starting to have fun again as we get busy making our costumes. We find cotton wool, paint it and tape it to our chins as scary hairy beards. (I colour mine red to match my hair. I actually look a bit like an old photograph I have seen of Daddy. When he was younger he had a fluffy red beard!)

Because I am the best at drawing I sketch our swords and eyepatches on black card and Marge cuts them out. We even make pirate jewellery out of some old buttons from Mummy's sewing kit.

Archie looks brave with his beard and hat but he refuses to wear the small black boots that I cut out for him.

Zara has the most terrifying costume because Marge manages to make a hook out of a plastic coat hanger and tucks it into her onesie. She keeps waving her hook hand at us!

Then we hear a loud raspberry sound which is followed by a foul smell in the air.

It seems to be coming from Zara.

PHEW EUK!

It stinks worse than broccoli and smelly socks.

Zara points to her nappy with her little hook hand.

'Captain No Beard did a doo-doo,' Jakey complains.

Marge looks worried. 'I wish we had the Royal Nanny here to help. I've never changed a nappy before!'

'Who changed the nappies at sea?' I ask.

Jakey is now holding his nose.

'Poop-Patrol Pete was in charge of Code Brown. He used his eyepatch to cover his nose,' Marge explains.

I have changed lots of nappies on my

dollies. And I did promise Mummy I'd help Marge today . . . I glance at Jakey, and I know he's thinking the same as me. We both love having Marge to look after us, even if it means we have to look after her a bit sometimes too.

'Don't worry, Captain. We will do it.' I pat her shoulder reassuringly.

'**Phew!** Good work, me hearties.' Marge the Pirate Nanny salutes us gratefully. She moves to the far side of the room, where she opens her umbrella and hides behind it. Archie's tail is between his legs.

'**Ewww-eeeee!**' shouts Jake as I take off the dirty nappy.

'I haven't smelt a poop this stinky since my gorilla Edwina overdid it on the cauliflower cheese,' Marge confides from behind her umbrella.

Jakey and I make a great team. He pulls faces at Zara to keep her calm (and because it smells so yukky) while I change her. We must look so funny to Zara – a pair of fierce scallywag pirates changing her nappy!

'**Yayaya!**' Zara points her hook hand at me and Jakey when we have finished.

'That means she likes us,' Jakey says.

I hope this means less biting and tipping things over us in the future.

As we're washing and drying our hands, I remember how sleepy Zara was earlier. 'Is there anything in the Pirate Code about bedtime for babies?'

Marge's face lights up. 'Yes, I forgot!'

Rule 6. All pirates need a ship deck to sleep on and the waves to rock them to sleep

'We are going to build a ship for Zara to sleep in,' Marge announces. 'That will fix her insomnia.'

We rush around constructing a life-size pirate ship that looks as much as possible like Jakey's Lego one. Zara is happily throwing the ball for Archie. She's really good at it!

'I'll fetch the sail.' Marge is running into the house, her magical hair fanning out behind her.

'Batten the hatches,' I shout. Together we drag an old wooden table under the shade of the oak tree and turn it upside down. Then we put a cardboard box on top of it.

We cut windows for the portholes and make an anchor out of Daddy's spanner and a skipping rope.

'Thar she blows!' Jakeypants the Fierce cries, as he hoists Marge's 'sail' onto a rake propped against the table. It looks a bit like the bed sheet from our parents' room.

'YOOYOO!' Zara cries, pointing to the mast and sail, which means (I hope) that she is finally ready to nap.

'All right – bedtime, little scallywag!' Marge tells her. She takes off Zara's hook and gently lays her on a blanket inside our 'ship'.

'She needs some booty!' Jakey runs off.

He returns from the house with Pete his stuffed dinosaur, and gives him to Zara to cuddle. I can't believe it!

So baby Zara snuggles Pete and closes her eyes, while Marge sings in her warbling cat voice.

'We love to sail the seven seas
Yo ho, yo ho,
a pirate's life for me
The ship's a place for sleepy babies
Yo ho, yo ho,
a pirate's life for me.'

Jakey and I tiptoe inside. I start drawing a picture of how I imagine Not-So-Jolly Roger to look. I draw his fingers and toes perfectly, and Jakey turns his Lego ship into a treasure chest.

After a while we get bored and sneak back to our ship. Captain No Beard is finally asleep. But where is Marge?

'Marge?' I whisper, peeping behind our ship.

But she doesn't reply.

Jakey checks the garden and even inside Zara's pram. We can't see her anywhere – our babysitter has disappeared! Suddenly I remember that the whole house is a mess from when Zara ran away, and from us creating our wonderful pirate costumes . . .

Just as I start worrying we hear a car in the driveway. **Uh-oh** – there's no time to find Marge now, and no time to tidy up! I hope Mummy understands that we couldn't do anything on her list because Zara ate it!

'Parents AHOY!' I call in my pirate voice.

If Marge hears me, she'll know that the grown-ups are home.

As Mummy and Auntie Sally walk towards us, smiling, Marge suddenly appears on the other side of the ship, where I was just looking a moment ago. Her pirate beard is gone and all her amazing hair is hidden away under her hat. Our pirate nanny looks like a regular babysitter again.

'Hi, Jemima.' Mummy gives me a hug. 'You look a bit like Daddy in that beard.'

Sally gazes at baby Zara dozing sweetly in our pirate ship under the tree. 'How was my darling baby-waby?' she asks.

'Marge was going to make Captain No Beard scrub the decks, but once we'd built her a ship she fell asleep. Everyone gets *out*somnia at sea!' Jakey informs them.

Mummy and Sally laugh, thinking he is being silly. If only they knew.

'Is that your dinosaur Zara is holding?' Mummy asks, surprised.

Jakey shrugs as if it's no big deal. Maybe my little brother is starting to like babies.

I think I am too. As I watch Auntie Sally gently picking up Zara and moving her back into her pram, I wish I could give her one last cuddle myself.

I sigh as we all head inside and then I remember the mess.

I am about to apologise, but when Mummy opens the door the entire house is SPOTLESS!

My mouth opens and closes like a goldfish's but no words come out. How is that possible? I look at Marge – is she magical? How did she manage to tidy up the whole house so quickly?

Marge gathers her bag and whispers to me, 'As shipshape as my shipmates,' as she heads to the door.

'How were the children? Did they behave themselves?' Mummy asks, looking at Jake and me expectantly.

Marge nods. 'They followed the Pirate Code well! Especially Code Brown.' She salutes us both farewell. 'Goodbye, Long

John Jemima and Jakeypants the Fierce. Only play with the blunt cutlasses and no rude words.' Marge winks at Jakey.

'What's Code Brown?' Mummy asks when Marge has gone.

'When Captain No Beard did a doo-doo and Jakey and I changed her all by ourselves!' I say proudly.

Mummy and Sally share a glance.

We all look at my baby cousin.

'ARRRRR!' cries Zara in her sleep, just like a real pirate dreaming of a battle.

Jakey and I stare at each other in shock. Maybe babies really are pirates at heart. I guess we'll never know.

Marge and the
Stolen Treasure

It was a boring and very hot day. Jakeypants (my four-year-old brother) and me (Jemima Button) were both in the garden. He was playing in a big cardboard box, but I could tell he was getting tired and sticky. I was reading my book in the shade. Not a single branch or leaf on any of the trees was moving. There were no clouds in the sky, and despite reading my book in the shade, I was sweatier than a polar bear on the beach.

DING DONG

Jakey and I look at each other. We aren't expecting any visitors today, are we?

'It's your babysitter, Marge,' Mummy calls as she heads to the front door. 'She's going to take you to the pool to meet your cousin Zara for a swim.'

YAY! I can't do a forward roll or click my fingers yet, but I am a really good swimmer. Mummy thinks that I could be part-dolphin because I can hold my breath underwater for so long. But wouldn't I be grey or have a fin? Jakey refuses to put his face underwater AT ALL. Or at least he used to.

We race inside. I am so excited. Marge is not a regular babysitter. She grew up in a palace with lots of amazing pets and doesn't act like a grown-up at all!

'MARGE!' we shout gleefully. She is standing in the doorway, no taller than a Christmas elf. Her hair is hidden in a swimming cap and she is wearing a pink dressing gown and gold sandals.

'Lords, ladies, gentleman . . . and animal friends,' she announces in a posh voice. Archie, our pug-nosed puppy, has appeared and yaps back at her. 'Prepare to swim with Margery Beauregard Victoria Ponterfois!'

She whips out a pink fan and wafts her face.

'Thanks for coming at such short notice, Marge,' Mummy says gratefully, and she heads back into the kitchen looking for something.

'My wombats are competing in the Marsupial Olympics, and Camilla Camel is getting a much-needed facial,' reveals Marge. 'So I had the afternoon free as it turns out.' She slides a sparkly key ring into her bag.

Mummy and Daddy are looking for their car keys because they have to go to the supermarket. Daddy's face is red.

'Jakey, have you hidden the car keys again?' he asks, sounding angry.

My little brother pretends not to hear. His new favourite game is hiding things. Yesterday he hid my crayons behind the radiator and last week I was searching

for my best purple socks for AGES before
Jakey confessed that he had buried them in
the garden. Mummy was furious when she
dug them up because they had a worm on
them, and I had to wear my sandals even
though it was raining.

'JAKEY!!'

Finally he admits they're in
the laundry basket. 'I am the best
hider ever,' he whispers to Marge.

'No, Princess Chantelle was the best
hider ever. She hid King Eugene's false teeth
and they were never found again,' Marge
whispers back. 'He could only eat jelly and
custard after that.'

Yum! I wouldn't mind that.

Mummy reminds Marge that her list is on
the fridge and that we have to behave nicely.
As we hug our parents goodbye, I act like I

will miss them, but secretly I won't. Having Marge around is the best fun in the world.

As the door shuts, Marge peels off her swimming hat and out flows her incredible rainbow hair. Then she whips off her robe and underneath she is wearing a polka-dot swimsuit!

'Get the list,' Marge orders, doing a high kick. 'Hop to it!'

Jakey mimes diving into a pool and then pretends to swim all the way to the kitchen. When he brings the list back, I read it aloud while Marge fans Archie, who is panting.

1 No swimming without sun cream or a hat

2. There are sandwiches and carrots for lunch

3. The pool is a 10-minute walk away, and clean towels are in the laundry basket

Jakey hates carrots so he takes the list from me and folds it in half, then into quarters. He keeps on folding until it's the size of a marble and hides it inside a matchbox. Mummy will not like that one little bit.

Marge flops into Daddy's chair and wipes her brow.

'I haven't been this hot since I galloped across the Arabian Desert on my black stallion, Sebastian Seranado.' She sighs dreamily. 'He was my first love . . .'

My beloved Sebastian ♥

'Why were you in the Arabian Desert?' I ask.

'I was on a royal expedition of course.'

'What is an expedition?'

'Explorers go on expeditions to Find
Things Out. To peer into unknown corners
of the world and discover new animals.'

Jakey jumps up and down. 'Can we go on
an expedition to the pool?'

Marge nods enthusiastically. 'Jemima,
you are head of the planning committee.'

I run for my silver notebook and the biro
with a feather on top.

'What do explorers need to take with
them?' My pen is poised.

'We will need . . .' Marge begins.

'A map?' Jakey pipes up. Even though
Jakey and I know the way to the pool,
Marge doesn't.

Marge nods her head and I write it down
in my Explorer's Notebook. 'A map can also
help explorers mark down new places and
creatures that they discover on their travels.'

Jakey finds a giant sheet of yellow cardboard and we draw our street, Wells Road. Marge sticks a gold star in the middle and labels it Jake and Jemima's place. I draw a miniature house nearby and mark it Lucy, Theo and Matthew's house. Last of all Jakey pours green glitter on a dab of glue at the bottom and writes Pool.

'Right, the next thing we need is some Marge's Marvellous Explorers' Lemonade,' Marge says, smacking her lips.

I don't know if Mummy will be happy when she sees that Marge has emptied all the tulips from the big blue china vase. Our babysitter is filling it with ice cubes and water to use as a jug!

We will have to be very careful. Sometimes Jakey accidentally smashes things. Like when he used Daddy's special red mug to smuggle dirt in from the garden. But I am having too much fun making the lemoniest lemonade to worry. We squeeze in lots of lemon juice and then it's ready.

'Let's taste it!' Marge pours us tall glasses and we clink them together. Then she insists that we all link arms and sip from each other's glasses. But we get in a terrible tangle!

My arm is somehow twisted around Marge's back, and Jakey's leg is over my neck and soon we look like a human octopus in a knot and our lemonade is spilling everywhere!

Marge glugs Jakey's lemonade . . . SLURP!

Jakey guzzles mine. FANTASTICO!

I gulp from Marge's glass. YUM!

Archie laps his up. LICK!

Packing for the expedition takes a little while. I can't find my swimming costume at first. It turns out Jakey has dressed Pete the dinosaur in it and then hidden him in the hallway closet. Then Marge mistakes Archie's dog blankets for the pool towels and packs Daddy's shaving cream instead of the sun cream.

I roll up our map, and put our lunch into Jakey's backpack. Around his neck Jakey is wearing our binoculars – we made them out of toilet rolls so we could spy on our parents during their dinner parties. (By the way, it turns out that nothing fun happens at dinner parties. They're not parties AT ALL. Grown-ups just sit, talk and eat.)

As we leave the house I grab our butterfly net, and we're off!

Marge has balanced the big china vase of

lemonade on Jake's red wagon. Jakey agrees he will pull it along the street . . . but he is not so agreeable on the subject of sun cream.

'It was on Mummy's list. You have to wear it!' I tell him.

Now, my little brother has two rules (as well as no sandpits or sharing his dinosaur):

1. He will never eat crusts. Even on pizza

2. He refuses to wear sun cream

Jakey looks determined as he shakes his head. 'NO sun cream. Ever.'

I am feeling upset now as I really wanted to go swimming, and everything else is ready. I am not crying but my eyes are starting to feel tickly.

Marge sees my face and thinks for a moment.

'All explorers need to be protected from wild animals. Did you know that sun cream scares tigers and lions away?'

Jakey looks surprised.

Marge continues. 'Jumping spiders are allergic to sun cream too.'

Jakey's eyes grow wider.

'And it's also been known to stop ladies from falling in love with you!'

'I want sun cream!' Jakey cries, slathering it all over his face and arms.

WHOOPEE!

At last we set off down the street. I am at the front, reading the map to help us find our way. Next comes Jakey, pulling along the red wagon with the huge vase wobbling on top. Archie trots behind us, his little paws moving quickly like he's a baby ballerina. At the back is Marge. She is using the binoculars to look for zebras and exotic plants and singing in her warbling voice:

'Explorers come from near and far,

Come by foot or come by car.

Today we adventure to the pool,

Let us be brave and keep our cool!'

During our walk we find an ant trail snaking along the pavement and into the long grass. Crouching down and using the binoculars, we manage to spot the ants marching through the blades of grass and up onto a tiny hill. There we discover the hole that leads to their underground world!

I peer inside. I would love to shrink down to the size of an ant, just for one day, to see what it's like.

'An explorer has to record what they discover,' instructs Marge.

So Jakey draws a picture on the map and I label it ANT CITY. Then I take my Explorer's Notebook out and sketch an ant wearing a top hat!

It is really hot and sunny, and the red wagon is quite slow on the lumpy pavement.

So we flop down outside Theo's house. Theo is Jakey's best friend and I am friends with Lucy, his big sister, but she is away at camp. Theo and his little brother Matthew run out to greet us.

'Where are you going?' they ask, eyeing our marvellous supplies.

'We are on an expedition to the pool!' Jakey explains in an important voice.

Theo is peering into the vase. 'Is that lemonade?'

Marge pours us all a drink. 'Explorers always share whatever they have on an expedition. When I was in Thailand I came across an orangutan named Oscar with terribly knotted fur. I shared the last of my shampoo with him. After a good scrub we combed out every single knot!'

Marge's face is so serious

when she tells us this that me and Matthew get the giggles.

When the lemonade is finished, it's time to be on our way. We wave goodbye to our friends and agree to meet them later at the pool.

The wagon is lighter now and easier to drag, until Archie, who is too hot to walk, jumps onto it and we have to pull him along as well. He curls up around the cool vase, napping.

We trundle on down the street. Marge is making bird calls with her hands, but to be honest she sounds more like an angry chicken squawking.

'At the palace we had an official Bird Whisperer called Augustus. Augustus could talk to any feathered friend, and he once saved four and twenty blackbirds from being baked in a pie. He taught me lots of bird calls.' She quacks loudly, like a duck. Then gobbles like a turkey.

Jakey snorts with laughter. The birds in the trees lining the street are curious however and circle us, chirping. I've never seen birds behave like this before. I am watching carefully so that I can write it all in my Explorer's Notebook later. But then Jakey joins in by howling like a wolf and they fly away!

'Maybe it was the sun cream that scared them,' he says with a shrug.

The others haven't noticed, but I have spotted a twig nest in the oak tree beside us. As I watch it, a tiny yellow beak pokes out. It's a baby bird.

'Look!'

They look where I am pointing and spot it too. Marge clucks to the bird for a long time.

'What are you doing, Marge?' I ask breathlessly.

'It's a prayer that the chick will learn to fly soon. That's what Augustus would do if he were here.'

I mark a tiny love-heart on the map where I saw the nest. I can't believe how lucky I am to have glimpsed a baby chick! I really am an explorer now.

The pavement leads us down to the main road. We're nearly at the swimming pool! There is a crossing ahead and Marge makes us wait, holding hands, looking left and right.

'Sun cream doesn't protect against speeding cars,' she says seriously.

We can hear shrieking and squeals of laughter as we round the bend and arrive at the entrance. The pool is shaped like a letter 'L' and there is an ice-cream shop and some shady trees to sit under too. The deep end has a diving board, and Lifeguard Steve sits next to it. He is short and round and shaped like a doughnut. Jakey calls him Shouty Steve because he always shouts instead of using his whistle. He didn't even blow his whistle a few weeks ago when Theo ate an ice cream *in* the pool. He shouted so loudly that day, I could hear him underwater.

Once we have parked our wagon and spread out the blanket under a big tree, we change into our swimming costumes. Then we hear a familiar voice . . .

'Goo-gaaah!'

I whip my head around. Our little cousin Zara (the naughtiest baby ever) is racing towards us in her swim nappy. She is wearing armbands, a blue blow-up ring around her middle and flippers on her tiny feet. Auntie Sally looks pooped, huffing and puffing behind her in a sun hat.

Zara only learned to walk recently so everyone thinks it's an 'accident' when she steps on our toes, but Jakey and I know differently.

'You're all here at last! Can you take my sweet angel for a dip while I change into my swimming costume?' asks our auntie.

She's got that wrong. Zara is no angel, she is a pirate baby who likes to make mischief.

'Of course,' Marge replies.

'I'll be back in five minutes!'

At the pool we dangle our legs into the cool water. It feels wonderful on such a hot day. Until suddenly I feel a pair of little hands on my back.

Zara just pushed me in! I have water up my nose . . . SPLASH

SPLISH

Jakey lands beside me in the water.

SPLOOSH

Marge is now sprawled on top of us!

Zara is smiling wickedly when we pop up, spluttering and bedraggled.

Marge swims over to the side and gives Zara's armbands a cheeky pinch. 'Explorers should always be prepared to expect surprises.'

SPLOSH

Marge has pulled Zara into the pool too!

Our little cousin is laughing as she bobs on the surface, splashing us.

Now Zara thinks this game is hilarious and wants to be pulled in again and again. Each time she kicks her legs and tries to make a bigger and bigger splash. It's fun at first, but after about twenty times it gets a bit boring.

'Did you know that I am in the royal synchronised swimming team?' Marge reveals, doing a showy somersault.

I hold Zara in my arms while Marge floats on her back and shows us her moves. She crosses and re-crosses her legs in the air while twirling underwater. She looks quite majestic in her polka-dot swimsuit, like a spotted sea lion performing tricks. Then my aunt shows up and takes Zara back. At last, I'm free to swim in the deeper water!

'Bye, Zara!' We wave cheerfully.

I swim over and see my friends Emily and Sarah jumping off the diving board. I wish I had the courage to do that, but I am scared of doing a belly flop in front of everyone.

Marge suggests that we play 'Explorers Looking for Treasure'. The game means swimming along the bottom of the pool to find coins and anything else people have dropped in the water by mistake. But Jakey is too scared. He hates getting his face wet.

'Real explorers go underwater,' I explain.

'Explorers often do things that they don't feel comfortable with,' agrees Marge. 'That's what makes them brave.'

Suddenly she has an idea. We watch as she darts over to her bag and comes back carrying a pair of strange-looking, very old goggles.

'These are my flying goggles,' she tells us, stroking them wistfully. 'When I flew over the Atlantic Ocean in my twin-jet plane *Aviator Marge the Fourth*, I used these goggles to keep the bugs from getting stuck in my eyelashes. All pilots need goggles – and sometimes explorers need them too.'

Jakey and I are gobsmacked. Marge is the most amazing adventurer!

I help adjust them to fit Jakey's head and, would you believe it, he ducks underwater and starts to swim!

I am so proud of him. I can't wait to tell Mummy and Daddy.

I show Marge my attempt at synchronised swimming, which is less majestic sea lion and more wriggly squid, while Jake uses the goggles to look for fish. Then together we search for treasure at the bottom of the pool.

Jakey and I find two coins, a single pearl earring and a hair clip with an orange plastic flower on the side. We take our pretty trinkets up to the surface, making a little pile on the side of the pool to take home.

When I come up for air again, I look over at Emily, who is now on the diving board doing a beautiful swan dive. I wish I could swan-dive from the diving board. Or even do a regular dive from there. I've practised lots of times from the edge of the pool.

Marge is watching me.

'Do you want to go on the diving board?' she asks, but I shake my head.

'What are you afraid of? You are my bravest explorer!'

'Everyone will stare at me,' I stammer. 'I don't know if I can do it.'

Her eyes light up and she swims over to me. 'I have a plan.'

Marge is going to create a 'diversion'. A diversion means that she will make lots of noise at one end of the pool so everyone will look towards her. At that exact time, I will try a dive from the diving board – without anyone watching me. My heart is thumping like crazy just imagining our plan in action.

Jakey is happy because Theo and Matthew have arrived. Matthew is scraping our butterfly net along the bottom of the pool to recover even more treasure.

Marge and I have worked out a special signal. When I tap my nose twice she will begin the diversion. My palms are sweaty as I jog across the scorching tiles to the

big silver diving board, passing Emily and
Sarah on the way.

As I climb up the steps I feel as nervous as
I did before the spelling bee. It's not *too* high
and the water looks blue and inviting but
everyone is staring at me. I inhale deeply,
then look over to Marge and tap my nose
twice. It's time for her 'diversion'.

She gives me the thumbs up. Then she makes a very loud oinking pig sound and starts thundering towards the water, shouting,

'BOOOOMMMBBBIIIEEEEEE!'

Marge leaps off the side of the pool, crunches her body up and hurls herself like a cannonball. She soars through the air and into the water, creating a massive splash. I hope Zara is watching.

Quickly I grit my teeth in determination as I put both my hands into a clap position, tuck my chin to my chest and dive neatly into the water.

SPLASH!

It feels so soothing in the cool pool and I pop my head up proudly. I can't believe it, but I did a dive from the board! All by myself. No one has noticed. They are all still shocked and spluttering from the tidal wave created by Marge's massive dive bomb.

Lifeguard Steve is totally drenched and his face is turning from pink to flaming red.

For the first time ever, he blows his whistle. He must be really angry. His cheeks are purple and bulging like a giant hamster.

Steve points to Marge and shouts, 'YOU, KIDDO, OUT OF THE POOL!'

WHHHEEEEEP!

Marge looks at me and taps her nose proudly as she pulls herself out of the water. Her bottom has eaten her swimming costume so everyone laughs as she heads over to Lifeguard Steve for a telling-off. I can see Jakey getting out of the pool too and standing up for Marge. I think he's also explaining that she isn't really a child but our small royal babysitter.

I am so astonished by my bravery that I quickly clamber up to try another dive, making my body even more streamlined by tucking my elbows in. I don't mind that everyone can see me now as I do another swan dive into the water.

SWOOSH!

I spend the rest of the morning trying different dives from the board. I can do a pencil dive, a starfish dive and a duck dive. Marge watches, giving me marks out of ten for each one until it's lunchtime.

'Ice cream first!' she cries, finding her wallet. 'An ice cream will help us get an appetite for lunch.'

I giggle. Mummy always says it's the other way round – that we need to eat lunch before we have a sweet treat – but Marge is in charge!

I choose a strawberry lolly and Jakey and Marge get mint choc chip ice-cream cones while Archie has to settle for a bowl of water. We flump back onto our blanket, next to my aunt and baby Zara. Sally tells us that Zara isn't allowed ice cream yet, but Zara is not pleased.

'GAAAA,' she growls, pointing at my ice lolly.

'No, not for you, my darling baby-waby. Have this!' my aunt pleads. She is trying to spoon apple sauce into Zara's closed mouth.

Suddenly Zara knocks the spoon so that apple sauce splashes on everyone. Auntie Sally is starting to look cross. As quick as her nimble little legs can carry her, Zara slips out of her mummy's arms and crawls over to Jakey. She grabs his ice cream and makes a dash for it. As she hurries away, she whips off her swim nappy and throws it defiantly into the air.

I chase after Zara, Jakey chases after me and Marge is right behind us. I think Auntie Sally is still in shock on the rug.

'NO RUNNING, KIDDOS!' shouts Steve.

We are finally able to corner our cousin near the entrance. We are all out of breath. The ice cream is melting down Zara's arm and she is wearing a naughty expression.

'Freeze, pirate baby!' I cry sternly.

'Give me back my ice cream,' Jake begs.

Zara shakes her head.

Marge talks to us in a calm voice.

'Explorers often meet different types of people who don't speak the same language. We have to find another way to communicate.'

I can see that Jakey would like to communicate by wrestling Zara, so I jump in quickly and try sign language (which I am learning at school), but Zara ignores me.

We both try miming, which is acting without words. Jakey pretends to be Zara and I pretend to be him, but Zara just looks bored.

Then I have the brilliant idea of swapping Marge's flying goggles for the ice cream.

Marge approves. 'Pirate babies love trinkets.'

Zara hands the ice cream over and puts Marge's goggles on. She looks like a big-eyed frog but at least she is happy. At last we all trudge back to the blanket. I'm pooped.

'Explorers often climb high trees so they can escape from wild animals and watch their enemies from afar,' Marge whispers to us.

'Good idea,' says Jakey. 'Zara is definitely a wild animal.'

First, though, Jakey and I need to hide our treasure. I lift up our blanket and dig a little hole in the ground. Then we wrap the coins and other bits up in our sandwich wrappers, bury the precious package and put the rug back on top.

'X marks the spot,' says Marge, so I take out our map and mark the hiding place with a giant X.

Luckily the tree we're sitting under has a wide base and long branches that are easy to swing onto. The leaves are like tiny umbrellas shading us from the sun. It's cool and dark up here. The middle branch is so wide that we can sit side by side on it. This is about as perfect a climbing tree as you could ever find.

Marge swings back down and up again, fetching our lunch.

Jake looks suspiciously at the carrots until Marge reminds him that explorers can't be picky eaters and then he gobbles everything up. Mummy will be so pleased.

From my high vantage point in the tree I can see Lifeguard Steve climbing down from his chair.

'Someone has stolen my whistle,' he shouts angrily. 'Whoever has taken it, please give it back!'

I see the tops of everyone's heads bobbing and weaving as they start searching everywhere. I wonder to myself if Jakey has hidden it, and I am about to ask him when I spot Mummy and Daddy over by the entrance.

Whoopee!

I never realise how much I have missed my mummy until I see her again. Auntie

Sally and Zara are making their way over to greet them.

We race down the tree as fast as we can, and together with Archie we run over for a hug.

Mummy goes to kiss Jakey but he pushes her away.

'I've got sun cream on, Mummy, so you can't fall in love with me today.' She laughs. 'I can swim underwater now too!' he brags. 'But only with Marge's flying goggles.'

'How was your swim, Jemima dolphin?' Mummy gives me a cuddle.

'Guess what?' I say shyly. 'I dived off the diving board. All by myself.'

Mummy and Daddy cheer loudly and Daddy ruffles my hair. 'Well done, Jem.'

'The children are truly fearless explorers,' Marge adds, looking proud and sensible with her rainbow hair hidden under her swim cap.

Is this really the same person who bombed into the pool oinking like a pig an hour ago?

Our parents explain that it's time to go home now so we need to fetch our things. Sally and Zara are going to walk with us.

'I want to show you our treasure first,' Jakey says.

'We found it at the bottom of the pool.' I unroll our map to show them the X. 'This is where it's secretly buried.'

We head off back to our camp under the shady tree to dig it up. But when we lift the blanket, the hole is empty. All our treasure is gone! Jakey and I stare at each other open-mouthed. Someone has taken our loot. But who? Nobody knew it was there. I look at Marge, who looks just as shocked as we are.

Daddy says we don't have time to search for it but promises we can find more treasure the next time we come swimming.

So we all walk home together. Jakey and I tell our parents about having a picnic in a tree and I show Mummy the drawings in my Explorer's Notebook. She really likes the one I did of the ant wearing a top hat. No one even asks why we are dragging a big blue china vase behind us on a wagon! Mummy is probably just relieved that Jakey didn't accidentally smash it.

When we get back to our house, it's time for Marge to head home too. She gives us a big hug as she rummages inside her handbag and brings out her sparkly key chain.

But the car keys are no longer on it!

'Jakey, have you hidden Marge's keys?' Daddy's eyebrows are raised, but my little brother shakes his head.

Slowly it dawns on me – I know who stole Marge's keys! I glance at Jakey and we both turn towards the one person we know who would steal treasure ... Zara the pirate baby.

Zara giggles and we notice that behind her back she is hiding her swim nappy. I can see that Mummy suspects her too.

'Please can I have that?'

Mummy tries to prise the nappy from Zara's grip and she resists. A tense tug of war follows, which Mummy finally wins.

She opens the nappy.

Marge, Mummy, Daddy, Sally, Jakey and I all GASP!

Inside is ALL our treasure, including the orange plastic flower hair clip, but also Marge's keys along with her magical flying goggles and, last but not least, Lifeguard Steve's whistle!

'You can take the baby off the pirate ship, but you can't stop her hunting for treasure!' Marge chuckles, shaking her head.

The grown-ups look a bit confused, but I couldn't agree more.

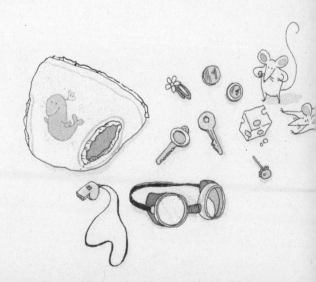

Marge and the Wacky Wedding

I wish you could see me right now. It's me, Jemima Button, and I am wearing a fancy yellow dress.

CLICK CLACK

My shoes have a tiny heel and make a tapping sound when I walk. I have a crown made of actual daisies too. Guess why? I am being a bridesmaid today! I can't wait. I have never been to a wedding before, except when I made my Barbie doll marry Jakey's dinosaur.

Jakeypants (my naughty little brother) is wearing a yellow suit and tie. 'I look like a banana,' he says crossly.

We are sitting on the front steps waiting for our babysitter, Marge. Mummy and Daddy have lots of jobs to do at the wedding, so Marge is coming to take care of us.

Are you wondering who is getting married? Well, it's Uncle Desmond and his fiancée, Annie. They fell in love and I think a wedding is what happens next. Jakey doesn't really understand weddings. He says that he loves Mummy and is going to marry her when he grows up. I am sure Daddy will have something to say about that.

Annie has pointy teeth, which is why Jakey nicknamed her 'Annie Alligator'. She babysat us once when Jakey was two and I was five, and my naughty little brother deliberately locked her in the bathroom and hid the key inside his shoe! I like Annie, but she hasn't babysat for us since. Which isn't a bad thing, I suppose, because now Marge is our babysitter and she is the most fun grown-up in the world.

Did you know that Marge is so small that she only comes up to Daddy's armpit? And she once cooked us chocolate soup for dinner.

Speaking of chocolate, at the party after the ceremony there is going to be a chocolate fountain! There will also be a band playing music and everyone will dance. I hope I get to dance with Daddy as he always lets me stand on his feet. We are allowed to stay up super-late and we don't even have to go to school tomorrow.

Did I tell you that I have a little wicker basket? It's filled with white rose petals that smell like summer.

We are supposed to scatter them on the bride and groom after the vows, so Jakey and I are practising on our puppy, Archie, while we wait for Marge to arrive.

'**Walkies**,' I call, and he trots towards us. We have handfuls of petals hidden behind our backs.

'**NOW!**' Jakey shouts, and we dump the petal confetti on Archie's head.

He keeps barking playfully at us and trotting away, but he always comes back when I call him. After a while we have to stop because we are running out of petals.

My little brother loves chucking confetti. I hope he doesn't get too excited and throw the whole basket at Annie's head.

Mummy has been getting ready for the wedding all morning. She has funny fat sausage curlers in her hair and she has even painted her toenails.

Daddy is with Uncle Desmond and his best man somewhere else. Uncle Desmond isn't allowed to see Annie before the wedding or it's bad luck.

I was so looking forward to today that I couldn't sleep last night. Then I had a nightmare that there was a spider in my bed. I woke Mummy up but she couldn't find it and was cross with me for making her tired.

Jakey has stomped off to tell Mummy his tie is itchy. He wants to take it off. I yawn and look up and down the street again, but there's no sign of Marge.

Then I spot a blurry red shape in the distance. It's a scooter, zig-zagging speedily down the street with a small person perched on the back.

That absolutely, most definitely, has to be Marge.

I run inside and find Jakey, who is burying his tie in the kitchen bin.

DING DONG

We race to the door. I can't wait for Marge to see us all dressed up.

WOW! Marge looks really smart and sensible today – apart from the glittery purple motorbike helmet on her head. She flips up the visor.

'Sorry I'm late. I was painting a portrait

of Natasha, my pot-bellied pig.' She gives us both a warm hug. Marge smells like a blown-out candle – it must be her scooter. 'You both look very dapper, as if you are off to a royal ball.'

'TIES ARE STUPID,' Jakey's voice booms. He is the loudest child in our school. I can hear him from my classroom, which is all the way at the other end of the building.

Marge takes off her helmet and pops it onto Jakey's head. 'Now no one will know it's you,' she tells him.

It's almost bigger than his body!

We both turn to stare at Marge. Her long rainbow hair is sculpted into a wave. She looks like a colourful cockatoo.

'Hi, Marge,' Mummy calls, heading for Jakey. She has rescued his tie from the bin. Mummy is the maid of honour, which is a very busy and serious job. She seems a bit stressed as she wrestles Jakey's tie back on.

'The list is on the fridge,' says Mummy, finally catching sight of our babysitter. 'What an unusual rainbow hat, Marge!'

Jakey and I share a look. We know that Marge isn't wearing a hat.

Marge smiles and does a little curtsy. 'I wore it when I was bridesmaid number twenty-nine for the Duchess of Winkerstink.'

Mummy laughs, and I can tell that she thinks Marge is joking about her royal connections. But Jakey and I know better.

'Well, thank you so much for coming, Marge. It's good to have such a sensible, reliable babysitter. Especially today.'

Jakey looks at me and rolls his eyes.

If there is one thing Marge is not, it's sensible. I once had to talk her out of building a tower with all our furniture. When Mummy is back upstairs, Marge describes how the Duchess of Winkerstink wanted to arrive at her wedding in a gold hot-air balloon. But after a breakfast of baked beans, she suffered a terrible bout of gas. Apparently her windy bottom pushed the balloon in the wrong direction and she crash-landed in Spain instead.

THE DUCHESS OF WINKERSTINK—
a wedding gone with the wind...

Would a sensible person say that?!

'Let's see Mummy's list,' Marge says, clapping her hands together. 'Hop to it!'

We mount our imaginary horses and gallop into the kitchen. My horse is a little slower so Jakey beats me and grabs the list.

Jakey is learning to read. Even though he says that he 'hates books' he actually read four pages of a chapter book yesterday.

'C'mon, Jakey, you can read the first line and I will read the rest,' I encourage him.

My little brother drops the paper to the floor and crosses his arms. 'NO!' This is clearly not one of his reading days.

'What are you doing up there?' asks Marge. She has the list and is crawling underneath the kitchen table. 'Indeed, no one can read a list unless they are inside the Reading Cave. C'mon!'

I lift up our tablecloth and peek at her. She is all scrunched up in a little ball and wearing a goofy smile.

'Do reading caves have bears?' asks Jakey.

'No. Bears prefer to eat books – not read them. Hurry up, there's only room for two more!' She pats the space next to her.

My brother ducks down and bunny-hops over to Marge. I crawl in behind him, thinking how clever our babysitter can be.

We move the chairs to close the cave up and sit beside Marge. She peers at the list and pulls her silver pen out of her bag.

'Help me with this bit, Jakey?'

And the next thing I know, my little brother has read three lines.

1. Please entertain the kids (and keep them quiet) in the back room until the ceremony begins

Marge opens her backpack and inside there are paints and crayons, beads and glitter. It looks as if she's packed a whole art cupboard.

'Every artist needs supplies,' she tells us. 'Today we shall paint the bride and groom in all their glory.'

Next to the first rule she writes: Paint all day.

I am so excited! I love painting, and art is my favourite subject at school. We read on:

2. Jemima and Jakey will walk down the aisle before the bride and groom

Now it's Marge who looks excited. 'All eyes will be on you, so be sure to smile as big as the moon and do jazz hands.'

We grin, and carry on reading.

3. Jemima will carry the rings on a little pillow and present them to the bride when the registrar calls the 'ring bearer'

'The ring bearer is the most important job at the wedding,' I explain. 'The rings are made of gold and must not be lost.'

Jakey nods seriously and Marge agrees. I am quite proud of being given such a big responsibility.

4. Do not let the kids near the cake or the chocolate fountain

Marge scribbles furiously. Now it reads, Let the kids swim in the chocolate fountain.

We both start to laugh as Marge mimes doing backstroke. Then Jakey 'swims' off towards the bathroom.

Marge winks at me. 'Let's finish the list.'

5. When the service is over, please encourage the kids to throw their petals gently at the bride and groom

Marge scribbles next to it and I read: Throw real roses, not just petals. It will be more dramatic!

'I don't know if that is a good idea,' I say. 'Thorns are sharp.' Marge looks disappointed, but she crosses it out and moves on.

6. Please help Jakey use a quiet voice during the service

We hear a flushing sound and he appears in the doorway.

'Did you wash your hands?' I ask.

'I won't!' Jakey insists, crawling back to us grumpily.

My brother has two rules:

1. He won't leave the house without his plastic sword

2. He hates washing his hands. He says it's 'boring' and that germs were invented by grown-ups to stop him having fun

Suddenly we hear Mummy dashing past. 'Where are the flower bouquets?' She sounds worried. 'They should be here by now.' She looks out of the window. 'We can't wait much longer or we will be late.'

'Don't worry, leave it to us,' Marge says. Mummy looks relieved and rushes upstairs.

'Ready, my little *artistes*?' Marge asks us.

So Jakeypants, Marge and I run around our garden collecting wildflowers. We find bluebells, daffodils, violets, poppies and lavender. Mummy sorts them into bunches and we tie them together with white ribbons. Some of Jakey's flowers still have roots, but Mummy is thrilled.

'Let's go!'

Mummy revs the engine as we all pile into our old blue car. I can't stop imagining what Annie will look like in her white dress. I have a sticker book on brides. Some ladies wear a long headdress made of lace called a 'veil'. I wouldn't want to wear a veil in case I looked like a ghost haunting a party.

Mummy leads us in a sing-along as we drive down our road and swerve round the corners, past the park, the greengrocer and the cake shop until at last we're at the town hall. This is it.

Inside, the hall is beautifully decorated with white roses and lilies. Mummy says they are Annie's favourites. Everywhere smells of flowers! There is a beautiful chandelier with lots of triangles of glass twinkling in the light.

My palms are starting to feel sweaty.

Today is a big day for me. Everyone is going to see me walk down the aisle and present the rings to the bride and groom. I hope I don't make any mistakes.

Mummy has to show people to their seats when they arrive. She points us to a back room where we can hide out until the wedding begins. That way, no one will see our special outfits until we walk up the aisle.

Marge flings open the door and we run around exploring.

'This will be our artists' studio!'

The room is empty except for a table holding a large glass bowl filled with mints. Jakey shovels some into his basket before Marge moves it away. I hide the ring pillow on the windowsill where it's safe.

WOOF WOOF

I catch Jakey's eye. I know that bark. We turn to see where the sound has come from . . . There's something wriggling under Marge's coat. Out pops Archie!

Oh no! Dogs are not invited to weddings.

Marge doesn't seem surprised. 'An artist needs a muse,' she says. 'He can be ours.'

Archie's tail wags happily as he covers my face in licks.

'What's a muse?' Jakey asks.

'A muse inspires artists. What shall we paint, Archie?' Marge asks our puppy.

I don't know if I told you this, but our babysitter can communicate with animals. She once helped a 130-year-old turtle make friends with a blind dolphin. Apparently the turtle would ride on the dolphin's back and shout, 'Go left,' or, 'Go right,' and they stayed together for ten years until one day the turtle fell off.

Archie yaps twice.

'Exactly!' Marge nods to Archie before explaining that our puppy wants us to decorate Annie and Desmond's car, so that the bride and groom can leave in style. I am impressed that Marge got all that from two yaps.

Marge pulls out her art supplies and tells us that Archie thinks we should paint streamers and make love-heart paper chains as decorations.

Archie is a brilliant muse. It will be the most special crazy car when we are finished, I can't wait to see Uncle Desmond and Annie's faces.

Then Theo and his little brother Matthew arrive with Auntie Sally and baby Zara.

'I don't think Zara will stay quiet during the vows. Can I leave her with you?' Sally asks Marge, plopping Zara in her arms.

Mummy told me that the 'vows' are the part where the bride and groom promise to be together for ever.

Zara is dressed up like an angel with a giant pink bow on her head. She tries to pull it off, but her mummy warns her, 'No bow, no go.' Then Auntie Sally pecks her daughter on the head, calls goodbye to her 'sweet baby-waby' and leaves.

Jakey and I glance at each other. We both know that our cousin isn't a sweet angel. We suspect she is actually a pirate baby! When her parents go to sleep at night Zara probably ransacks the house and makes her toys walk the plank. She certainly knows how to make a mess.

'Ga-ga!' she cries, pointing at Marge and grinning, her one sharp tooth glinting like a dagger. Jake is happily painting blue stars but I am feeling a little bit nervous. Zara is definitely the kind of baby who could ruin a wedding. Mummy told me that getting married is one of the most special days in a grown-up's life. I look at Theo and Matthew, who are fighting over the stapler. Zara is trying to reach for the scissors, and Jakey and Archie are playing fetch with a glue stick. How is Marge going to stay in charge of us all today?

She seems to read my thoughts and smiles. 'You can't be worse than bonobo chimps,

Jemima. And I took five of those to tea at the Dorchester Hotel once. Chimps are just like children. They also like to fling their own poop.'

But she has spoken too soon, as at that moment Zara paints a black moustache on my pink love-heart! I feel my eyes tickle with tears. Zara is the meanest pirate baby ever! I know that she did it on purpose.

I run to the bathroom and try to wipe the paint off with toilet paper, but it doesn't work.

Marge appears holding a bottle from her bag. 'Try Marge's magic paint potion,' she suggests. 'I never leave home without it.'

We squirt it onto Marge's paintbrush – **SPLODGE!** It is bright green and sticky.

Is this really going to help? I wonder.

Marge sees my face and laughs.

Slowly I dab at my painting with the brush of green goo . . . and the yucky black moustache washes away! My love-heart is still there underneath, looking perfect.

PHEW!

Back in the main room, Zara is pulling the tops off felt-tip pens and throwing them at the boys.

'When does the wedding start?' I ask.

Marge runs to the window. 'Now! The bride is arriving. Hide the decorations!'

We all tidy our art away and I wash my hands just in time. Annie has appeared at the door. I gasp. She looks like a human marshmallow, but also beautiful. Jakey is so excited that he runs over and hugs her.

Annie smiles. 'Hello, Jake. I just came to use the bathroom. I'm a bit nervous.'

Marge nods and points her towards it.

Oh NO.

Jakey didn't wash his hands. He has left two bright blue handprints on the back of Annie's dress!

Annie has to walk down the aisle in a minute. Luckily she hasn't noticed . . . yet. Marge's mouth is wide open in a perfect 'o' shape. She seems to be frozen in shock.

GULP!

A bride can't wear a dress with blue paint on it, can she? My mind begins to race with ideas. Maybe we can borrow a dress from Mummy. Or hide it by decorating it with flowers.

My heart is hammering in my chest. If only Jakey had washed his hands.

Jakey looks sheepish as he waits at the bathroom door.

'Don't tell me that you are thinking of locking her in there again,' I warn him. 'We can't kidnap the bride from her own wedding!'

'I'm sorry,' he sniffs. 'I promise I'll wash my hands next time! I didn't mean to ruin her dress.'

The toilet flushes and Annie comes out smiling.

'She hasn't seen the paint,' Jakey whispers in astonishment.

'She must be too nervous to notice,' I marvel.

'I couldn't help it. I was just so excited to see her,' he sniffs.

Now Mummy rushes in. 'The guests are seated,' she tells us, smiling at Annie. Luckily for us she hasn't spotted the blue paint either.

I hear the organ begin to play 'Here Comes the Bride'.

What should I do? A part of me thinks that I should tell Annie because walking down the aisle with blue handprints on her bottom would be embarrassing, but another part of me thinks of what Daddy always says: 'What you don't know can't hurt you.'

So I fetch my flower basket and brush my hair. As we all head into the hall, I suddenly remember number three on Mummy's list.

I am the ring bearer! When people get married they give each other rings so everyone knows they're husband and wife.

I race back to the windowsill, but would you believe it? The gold rings and their pillow are GONE. I am panicking. My stomach is churning like a washing machine. I look . . .

UNDER the chairs,

BEHIND the curtains,

IN the bathroom,

. . . but I can't find the rings anywhere.

I have lost them!

It's nearly time for Annie to walk down the aisle. Jakey and I are supposed to walk in front of her. But I am in the back room looking for the rings!

I feel tears coming. There is only one person who can help – Marge. She is standing in the doorway, watching me race around. She seems worried too. I am about to cry.

'Marge,' I panic, 'I have lost the rings!'

'Jemima...' Marge confesses, her rainbow-wave hairstyle beginning to droop sadly, 'I have lost baby Zara!'

Well, I don't need to be a detective to work out this puzzle. Baby Zara has stolen the rings and run away! Everyone knows that pirate babies love trinkets. I am sure if we find that one-fanged baby thief, we will find those rings. We dash about madly looking for Zara, but she is nowhere to be seen.

Marge heads outside as I run all the way to the back of the hall to find Jakey. Maybe my little brother can help us. Just as I arrive, the organ song gets even louder as if it's telling us to hurry up.

'We have to go NOW!' Jakey tells me.

He grabs my hand and drags me forward. We are going to lead the procession; that's what bridesmaids and pageboys do.

At the back of the grand room, Annie is standing with her father. Mummy waves at us proudly from her seat. She nods at me to signal that it's time to set off, just as we practised. I take a deep breath and try to think calm thoughts. Slowly Jakey and I start walking down the aisle in time to the music.

All I can see are lots of faces and weird lady hats, but then I see Granny and Grandpa

so I wave to them. Jakey spots Theo and Matthew's daddy in a pinstriped suit. Before we know it we have finished the walk. Together we turn back to face everyone and smile as big as the moon and do jazz hands, just like Marge told us to.

Annie is also smiling from the back of the room. She looks like a princess in her wedding dress. It is pearly and as fluffy as a cloud.

Uncle Desmond's eyes are so happy.

But I am still scared. My heart is pounding in my ears. What will happen when they ask me for the rings? I can't believe Jakey and I have ruined Annie's big day.

I am so full of my own thoughts I barely notice people whispering and nudging each other. But as Annie walks up the aisle, the sounds grow louder. Then I see people sniggering and hiding their snorts of laughter behind their hands. Lucy's mummy and Mabel look perplexed. What is going on? Even Daddy is frowning in confusion.

Now I see why.

Walking behind Annie, as she glides down the aisle, oblivious to the giggles, is tiny Marge. And she is holding her paintbrush! She is dabbing the back of the bride's wedding dress with the magic green goo potion that removes paint.

What a good idea, Marge!

Luckily Annie is too happy to notice, and before they reach the front Marge ducks behind a pillar.

Annie stands and faces her husband-to-be, looking radiant. Her dress is white again, the blue handprints completely gone.

Jakey nudges me. Because we are very close, I can see a tiny damp patch on Annie's dress where the creamy satin has turned see-through. Jake and I can see Annie's underwear!

He whispers to me: '"Annie Alligator" just became "Annie Underpants"!'

For the first time I forget about the missing rings. In fact I nearly collapse in giggles, but then I see Mummy looking at us and I stand nicely. I turn my body away from Jakey because I mustn't laugh.

Now the registrar is talking. He has a moustache that twitches when he speaks.

I really hope he doesn't get angry at me in front of everyone when he realises that I have lost the rings.

'Do you, Desmond Button, take Annie Nutley to be your partner in life, to love and cherish through good times and bad?'

My uncle says, 'I do,' and smiles at Annie.

While everyone gazes happily at the couple, I turn around and sneak a peek for Marge. And I spy her whizzing across the back of the hall as fast as her short legs can carry her!

The registrar turns to Annie Underpants and says, 'Do you, Annie Nutley, take Desmond Button to be your partner in life, for richer and poorer?'

I pretend to scratch my neck so I can turn round again. This time I glimpse Marge running in the other direction.

'I do,' Annie says as she gazes into my uncle's eyes. I can see that they are very much in love. I can't wait to be a bride one day.

'Who is the ring bearer?' the registrar asks, looking in my direction.

I don't know what to do, so I stare at my shoes and gulp.

Everyone is looking around and the registrar clears his throat. 'Where are the rings? Who has them?' he asks again.

My face grows hot and red. Jakey nudges me and I can see Mummy is staring at me too.

'Grrrrr!' growls a voice loudly behind us.

Zara is holding the ring pillow as she speeds down the aisle with Marge in hot pursuit.

PHEW

'THAT SMALL BUT DANGEROUS PIRATE is the ring bearer!' Jakey shouts in his outdoor voice, pointing at Zara.

The registrar looks surprised.

Everyone's eyes are now on Zara.

She pauses and gives an adorable smile while trying to find an escape route.

Now Archie bolts down the aisle.

WOOF WOOF

Mummy's face is beginning to go as green as Marge's magic potion. Our puppy gallops past Daddy, who tries to catch him but misses. Archie bounds over to Zara and grabs the ring pillow in his jaws.

'Wait, is *that* the ring bearer?' The registrar looks confused as he points to our puppy.

'No, that's our muse,' Jakey corrects him.

'Walkies,' I call, and Archie trots towards me. I reach out and grab the pillow just as Marge scoops Zara into her arms and vanishes out of the hall.

'I am the ring bearer.' I grin triumphantly, holding up two gold wedding bands.

Everyone in the hall is now on their feet, cheering and clapping like it's a concert! **'ARGH-HAA!'** I can hear Zara's piratey voice in the distance.

Eventually all the grown-ups settle down.

I have never been as relieved in my life as when I hand over the rings to the registrar.

'Is there anyone here who knows any reason that these two people should not be married? If so, please speak up now.'

Everyone is silent and I look out at my mummy and daddy, who both have happy tears sliding down their faces. Grandpa and Grandma are holding hands and Auntie Sally and Uncle Nick are sharing a smile. Just when I am thinking that the wedding is now going very smoothly, my little brother stands up.

'I HAVE A REASON,' announces Jakey in his outdoor voice.

Instantly the room is absolutely silent.

Everyone is looking at Jakey, at both of us. What is he going to say?

The registrar looks confused. 'Go on, what is the reason?' he asks.

'She looks like a marshmallow!' Jakey jokes, pointing at Annie.

Everyone gasps in surprise . . . but luckily Annie throws back her head and laughs and laughs. And then the whole hall joins in! Mummy and Uncle Desmond and everyone – even the registrar – are chuckling and smiling and giggling. Dear old Mabel nearly rolls out into the aisle. Mrs Beacher knocks her own hat off, she is laughing so hard.

Once everyone has settled down, again, the registrar puts his hand on the shoulders of Annie and Uncle Desmond. 'Finally . . . you may kiss the bride!' He wipes his brow and sighs with relief.

Uncle Desmond takes Annie Underpants's face in his hands and kisses her gently.

I whisper to Jakey that we can throw our rose petals now.

Everyone cheers as we sprinkle the bride and groom with confetti, but suddenly we hear . . .

'OW!'

'STOP!!'

'OUCH!'

Jakey is throwing the hard mint sweets that he snuck from the bowl earlier. They're raining down on the bride and groom like little stones!

'Sorry, I ran out of petals,' Jakey explains.

He scampers round picking up the mints
and trying to eat them until Mummy pulls
him away. Poor Jakey cannot control himself
when he gets excited.

Right after that we get to go into another
grand room, with fairy lights on the ceiling.
There are lots of white tables and chairs
and a chocolate fountain and a band. Marge
explains that if we get split up, we have
to meet back at the chocolate
fountain for a midnight swim.

Jakey, Marge, Archie and I have the best
time (once Jakey has taken off his itchy
tie and baby Zara has fallen asleep in her
pram). We crawl around beneath the tables
while the boring speeches are happening
and then we sneak three giant slices of cake
under there and have a picnic. As we guzzle
the yummy food, Marge entertains us with

stories of the Duchess of Winkerstink's wedding extravaganza.

When the band starts playing it's too loud for us to hear each other, so we all have a boogie. I am doing silly star jumps with Mummy until Daddy lets me dance with him, standing on his feet.

Jakey, Theo and Matthew look like kangaroos doing karate as they hop and chop the air.

And Marge and Archie are doing the tango.

It's the best party that I have ever been to. And the only time I have ever seen grown-ups having so much fun. Later on we sneak out to Uncle Desmond's car and start covering it with our decorations. I put streamers on the roof and we all throw confetti and stick our pictures on the dashboard. Jakey puts the rest of his sweets on the front seat. You should see Annie Underpants and Desmond's faces when they spot their car. They look so happy!

Although Uncle Desmond's face is a little less happy when he sits down on the hard sweets.

Ouch!

But no one is cross with my little brother. He has helped to make their wedding day extra special. And even though we made a few mistakes, I think that being a bridesmaid has been the best job ever. I can't wait to get married when I grow up.

I'm sure you're wondering if we ever swam in the chocolate fountain. Well, I am not going to answer that in case Mummy and Daddy read this story, but let's just say . . . I still have chocolate behind my ears!

Marge and the Missing Tooth

'COME OUT!' I say.

My four-year-old brother is hiding under his bed.

'Marge is here!' I am so happy.

Marge, the best babysitter in the whole universe, is at our house and my little brother doesn't care. I don't know what is wrong with him. Marge is not like a normal, boring babysitter. Marge is just the opposite: she is a member of the royal family and she once helped us build a dinosaur out of pancakes.

Mummy and Daddy appear in the doorway looking smart. Daddy is in a suit and Mummy is wearing a fancy black top.

'We have to leave for the party now. Please come out,' Daddy begs.

'NO!' Jakey sounds cross. This is not like him at all. Usually when he hears that Marge is coming he pulls his shorts over his head like a wrestling mask and races to the door to greet her.

I walk with our parents to the hallway where Marge is waiting. I always forget how small she is. Even though I am only seven years old, I am nearly as tall as our grown-up babysitter. She can even fit inside our play tent without bending over.

Today she is wearing a shiny silver shirt and a strange silver hat.

'Greetings, earthling,' Marge jokes, giving me a robotic wave. She does look a bit like she has come from outer space, and I giggle.

'We won't be back until late.' Daddy gives me a hug. 'And remember, Marge is in charge!'

'See if you can cheer Jakey up,' Mummy says as she grabs her car keys. 'He's been under that bed since he got home from school.' Then, as she is half out of the door, she remembers. 'I left the rules on the fridge.'

Usually Marge adds things to Mummy's rules to make them more fun, like the time when she took us to Theo's birthday party. Marge changed Mummy's rule about only eating one slice of cake at the party to *nine* slices!!

The minute we have waved off our old blue car Marge does my favourite thing. She takes off her hat and shakes out her long rainbow hair. It is so crazy – red, green, yellow, orange and blue.

'Let's go cheer up your brother!' Marge dances down the corridor and into our bedroom. I am getting very mad at Jakey; it's so exciting to have Marge here and all he is doing is hiding and spoiling the fun.

I want Marge to tell us wild stories about when she lived in the palace or travelled the world with her fourteen pets.

'Jakey?' Marge pretends she can't see his legs poking out from underneath the bed.

'Yoo-hoo,' she calls, checking behind the curtains and inside my closet.

'Where are youuuuuu?' she sings.

'I'm under here,' a little voice replies.

Marge hoists up her skirt and crawls under his bed. I wriggle in after her until we are both facing Jakey.

My brother's face is blotchy and red.

'Whatever is the matter?' Marge asks. 'I haven't seen such a sad face since the Marquis of Humperdink played tennis in the ballroom and smashed his favourite Ming vase.'

'My tooth won't come out.' Jakey's bottom lip is quivering. 'I've had this stupid wobbly tooth for so long and it won't budge!'

'That is terrible news.' Marge looks grave.

'Theo has lost a tooth and the tooth fairy gave him a whole pound!' Theo has one long eyebrow and is Jakey's best friend from school.

'The tooth fairy is never going to visit me,' Jakey whimpers.

'Never say never, Jakeypants,' Marge tells him. 'I remember when I thought I was never going to see my hairy-nosed wombat George again after he buried himself underneath the castle moat, but then, one day, there he was! Sunning himself on the Queen's lounge chair, drinking tea and wearing her missing tiara.'

Marge shuffles closer to Jakey. 'Can I see?' She gently wobbles his tooth with her finger.

'I've tried pulling it out,' Jakey sniffs. 'I've wiggled and pushed, but it's stuck.'

'Dentist Marge to the rescue!' Marge exclaims, and at last Jakey smiles. 'All we need is your daddy's toolkit.'

The smile runs away from my little brother's face, and he looks a bit frightened as we all crawl backwards out from under the bed.

Then Marge tells me that I will be the dental assistant, which I am actually quite excited about.

'I once removed my Persian cat, Amelia's, left fang, after she broke into the palace larder and ate too many sweets. It was rotten to the core!' Marge tells Jakey. 'I also pulled a tooth that had been stuck in a suit of armour in the castle for a thousand years. The knight didn't feel a thing!'

I run to the garage and come back with Daddy's toolbox and Marge whistles as she searches through it. I have the brilliant idea that we might need protective gear in case there is blood, so I grab an apron from the kitchen.

'Lie down,' I tell Jakey, as Marge puts on a gigantic pair of goggles.

'open up! WIDE.'

Marge and I peer at Jakey's teeth. They are white and pearly, and even though Mummy always says that he doesn't brush his teeth for long enough, they do look quite sparkly.

The toolbox is red and shiny and it has lots of weird and wonderful things inside it.

'Too big ...' Marge shakes her head as she pulls out a spanner.

'Too heavy . . .' Marge puts the hammer back.

'Too screwy . . .' She dismisses the screwdriver.

'Voila!' she grins, waving a pair of green pliers.

'Perfect!'

In case you don't know, pliers are like metal claws used for gripping things.

I am not sure what Marge is going to do with the pliers exactly as I have only seen Daddy use them to pull nails out of the fence, but I am just the dental assistant, not the dentist. I also have a small worry that our parents might not be very happy if they could see us now, but it was Mummy who told us to cheer up Jakey and he is definitely being cheered up, because even though he is scared, Jakey loves having people fuss over him.

'Maybe you should close your eyes,' I suggest, and he shuts them tight.

'Eenie, Meanie, Minie Mo,
This little tooth has got to go!'

Marge sings as she leans over Jakey.

357

She grasps the loose tooth with the pliers and braces her leg against the side of the bed.

'ARGHHHHH!'

Marge has fallen backwards and landed with her bottom in the air, but the tooth is still *inside* Jakey's mouth.

'The tooth is too wet for the pliers to grip onto,' I say, deciding that I am really good at being a dental assistant.

'No, it must be superglued in!' Jakey sits up.

Then I have the most obvious idea. I can't believe that I hadn't thought of it before. Jakey just needs to eat an apple! That's how I lost my tooth. But then I remember my little brother has two rules:

1. He will only eat his dinner if there is a pool of tomato ketchup in the centre of his plate that his veggies can 'swim' in

2. He hates apples. He won't eat an apple since the day he found out that worms can live in them

'You have to eat an apple to make your tooth come out,' I tell Jakey, and to my surprise he bolts into the kitchen.

Marge and I share a look as Jakey holds out a big green apple and then takes an enormous bite.

CHOMP!

He chews a bit and swallows.

'It's still the same amount of wobbly,' Jakey sighs. 'And this apple definitely tastes of worm poop.'

After that we tie a piece of string around Jakey's tooth and onto Archie's collar (Archie is our pug-nosed puppy dog) and try to get him to go for a run, but he won't and we are close to giving up when . . .

'I've got it!' I point to Jakey's remote-control monster truck parked in the kitchen doorway.

Jakey and Marge look at it too. Silently we nod our heads in agreement.

I tie the string around Jakey's tooth and Marge fastens the other end to the back of the truck.

Jakey has the controls. He looks determined as he pushes the control to Forward.

The truck takes off, shooting across the floor and the string grows taut . . .

POP!

Jakey's tooth flies out of his mouth. It's still attached to the string.

FINALLY!

Jakey grabs his tooth and we all race to the hallway. In the mirror I can see that there is a big hole where Jakey's wobbly tooth used to be! Jakey whoops with joy. I really am a great dental assistant.

'I remember when my long-toothed ferret Burt lost his first tooth,' Marge says proudly. 'We put it at the end of his bed – it was too long to fit under his pillow – and the tooth fairy brought him five hundred pounds. Long-toothed ferrets' teeth are extremely valuable.'

'The tooth fairy will be in our room tonight.' I am jumping up and down. This is almost as exciting as the time she visited *me*. Jakey gives Marge a big hug. I told you Marge is the best babysitter in the whole world.

'All right, let's read your mummy's

instructions.' Marge claps her hands. 'Hop to it!'

So we all take a careful look at the list of rules Mummy has left for us:

1. Dinner at 6.30 p.m.

2. Bath time — no need to wash hair

3. Brush teeth before bed!

4. Lights out at 8 p.m.

Marge checks her watch. 'It's 6 p.m. now so we have plenty of time before lights out.'

I am so happy Marge is here and Jakeypants is no longer Grumpypants! My little brother names his tooth Tim, and Tim the Tooth takes part in all our games and even comes to dinner. It's so much fun having a tooth to play with. Tim can ride in tiny cars, he can fly to the moon in our Lego rocket, he can sleep in a matchbox and he can even be a pretend pearl in our underwater diving game. In between activities Marge reminds Jakey to wrap Tim the Tooth in a little bit of tissue and keep him safely inside his pocket, but after our bath Jakey feels in there for Tim and screams.

'ARGGHHHH!'

'Where is my tooth?' he cries.

Marge and I peer into the empty tissue.

Oh no! What a disaster. After all that, we have lost the tooth.

'Mummy always says that when you lose something, you need to think about where you had it last,' I say. Marge nods in approval and we both look at Jakey.

'When did you last play with Tim?' I ask.

'I can't remember!' he groans.

'Did you bring Tim the Tooth in the bath?'

'I don't know!' Jakey sighs.

We check in the bathtub just in case, but NO TOOTH.

'Did you have Tim when we brushed our teeth?'

'I just can't think!' he exclaims.

'Maybe you swallowed Tim!' I gulp, and Jakey begins to cry.

Marge puts her ear close to Jakey's tummy.

'Interesting,' she says. 'I hear some fish fingers swimming around in there, and some broccoli . . .'

'That's just what we had for dinner,' I say. Can Marge really hear Jakey's food inside his tummy?

'And some apple juice,' she calls out. 'BUT I DO NOT hear a tooth!'

'Phew,' says Jakey. But he is only relieved for a minute.

'Maybe Tim fell down the sink!' he gasps.

We all three peer into the plughole. It is too dark to see anything. If Tim the Tooth is down there, he is lost forever.

'If we don't find him, the tooth fairy won't come!' wails Jakey. This is getting serious.

Marge runs downstairs and comes back
with Daddy's toolkit. She digs around a bit
and pulls the spanner out again. Then she
crouches under the sink and puts the spanner
around the pipe there and we all help her
turn it round and round and round.

'Tim is probably in the first part of this piping here,' Marge says. 'I've seen Petunia the palace plumber do this before. You just twist and twist . . .' she natters away.

Clunk!

A section of the pipe falls to the floor. Inside it we find a blue marble, a wand from a bottle of bubble mixture and a disgusting clump of hair. NO TOOTH. And now I can look down the plughole and see the floor. Mummy and Daddy will not like this!

'Your tooth must be further down!' calls Marge as she begins unscrewing more pipes.

'But, Marge,' I say, 'isn't that where the water comes from?'

Before Marge can answer, water starts squirting out of the pipe right into her face.

'**We've sprung a leak!**' she
shrieks.

Water is spraying all over the bathroom.

'Can anyone see Tim the Tooth? I hope he
can swim,' Marge calls.

'We can't see anything,' Jakey and I say as water spurts everywhere. I have to think fast. I grab the tube of toothpaste and force it inside the end of the leaking pipe.

'That'll hold,' says Marge in relief.

But I am not sure: the pipe is clanging and banging and quaking and shaking.

'What about my TOOTH?' yells Jakey again. 'If Tim didn't go down the plughole, then WHERE IS HE?'

I can tell he is about to cry when suddenly –

BRRRING

BRRRRING!

The sound is coming from Marge's bag!

'My alarm clock! It's eight o'clock!' gulps Marge. 'We have to put the LIGHTS OUT. That's what it says on Mummy's list!' Marge leaves us in the bathroom and we can hear her turning off the lights all around the house, *click, click, click*. It is getting dark, but Jakey hardly notices.

'Eight p.m. and the lights are OUT!' Marge says, taking a torch from Daddy's toolkit. 'We are following your mummy's rules PERFECTLY!'

I am not sure how destroying our bathroom fits into following Mummy's rules perfectly, but Marge is in charge.

'Now I miss my wobbly tooth,' Jakey sniffs. 'It was better than having a lost-forever tooth.'

'Detective Marge to the rescue,' Marge says seriously, while making swooping patterns with the torch.

'So tonight at approximately 7.30 p.m. was the last time we saw this missing tooth?' Marge asks Jakey, shining the torch on his face. He nods yes.

Marge still has Mummy's list of rules. She turns them over and together (like proper investigators) we work out everything that we did until then . . .

1. Made a traffic jam with toy cars

2. Ate dinner

3. Built a fort

4. Had a bath and brushed our teeth

5. DISCOVERED TIM THE TOOTH WAS MISSING!

'We have to do it all again, but backwards!' declares Marge. 'That's the only way we'll find Tim. Let's start with the fort.'

I love building forts, and Marge is *very* good at it because of the time she helped the King build a new wing onto the palace to make room for the Queen's chocolate collection. Our rebuilt fort is even better than it was the first time round. Jakey makes wings for it out of cushions and we fly over the kingdom in search of the missing tooth while Marge sings in her warbling voice.

'Toothy, middle bottom-left tooth,
You are in Jakey's mouth no more,

It's like you vanished with a poof.
Where you are, we can't be sure.'

But after all that there is still NO TOOTH.

'You played with Tim at dinner!' I remember. 'We popped him in the pea bowl so he could play hide-and-seek with some friends his own size.'

We race into the kitchen and Marge swishes the apple-juice bottle (we had let Tim take a swim in there) and Jakey checks the floor (Tim the Tooth enjoyed some tobogganing on the back of an ice cube earlier), but still there is NO TOOTH.

Jakey's shoulders are beginning to sag. I haven't seen him this gloomy since he wasn't allowed to watch *The Lego Movie* because Mummy thought he was too young.

'Don't give up, Jakey. There's still the traffic jam,' I say.

We arrange the cars in a long line, like we did earlier. We make the vehicles reach out of the playroom, down the stairs and under the dining-room table. It's so much

fun because Marge doesn't believe in speed limits or keeping to one lane and so all the cars shoot and skittle across the floor.

The whole time we make the cars shout at each other: 'Hey, Lady Chittleham, have you seen a tooth?! . . . Tell your driver to slow down!'

Jakey and I make our cars honk A LOT!

In between shouts and beeps we check each car and the floor very carefully. I look inside Jakey's fast red car twice, because I remember Tim speeding over a cricket-bat bridge in it and crashing into the sofa.

But there is NO TOOTH.

By now it is getting dark and I say a tiny prayer that if we can just find Jakey's tooth then I will never sneak Jakey's sweets from his secret box ever again.

'Right,' says Marge with a sigh, 'there is only one thing left to do.' She reaches into her bag and pulls out the spanner. She opens her mouth wide and puts it around one of her front teeth.

'What are you doing, Marge?' I gasp. But it's clear: she is going to pull out one of her own teeth!

'You need a tooth, Jakey,' says Marge, lowering the spanner. 'The tooth fairy won't care if it is yours or mine. She only pays attention to rare items like long-toothed ferrets' teeth.'

'But, Marge,' I say, 'haven't you already lost your teeth?'

'Yes,' says Marge, 'I lost one in a sword fight with the Grand Duke of Nottingham over the last slice of lemon-meringue pie . . .

A TOOTH FOR A MERINGUE

And I chipped one on the throne during an acrobatic performance with a one-legged duck.'

Marge starts to tug.

'**It won't grow back,**' shrieks Jakey in horror, but I can tell he is also a little bit excited. 'You'll look like a pirate . . . Or a baby . . . Or a . . . WITCH!'

Marge tugs harder. She really is going to pull out her tooth! I stare at my feet. I can't look.

'Wish me luck!' Marge says, just as I remember something.

'WAIT!' I scream. 'I saw Tim the tooth!'

Marge pauses as I close my eyes and try hard to picture what happened. As I was putting on my pyjamas with the daisies on the pockets, I saw Jakey putting his tooth under his pillow!

I hurry to get all my words out.

'OH YES, I forgot!' Jakey gasps. 'I put it there for the tooth fairy to collect.'

My little brother is only four, so he can't be expected to remember everything. We all bolt back upstairs into our bedroom and under Jakey's pillow we find . . .

Something small and white and just the size of a tooth!

Jakey grabs it and holds up his right arm like a champion.

'Hooray!' He kisses the tooth.

We did it!

'You saved the day, Jemima,' says Marge. But I think she is the brave one. She was going to pull out her grown-up tooth for Jakey!

Then Marge yawns. 'When do the chambermaids come to tidy up?'

She always forgets that we are not royal and we do not have servants. I start to worry. What will happen when Mummy and Daddy see the flooded bathroom?

The clanging, banging noise that started when I plugged up the pipe is *very* loud now. It sounds like a whale is trapped behind the bathroom wall, trying to get in.

Luckily for us, Marge has a plan. We leave Jake's tooth under his pillow with this note:

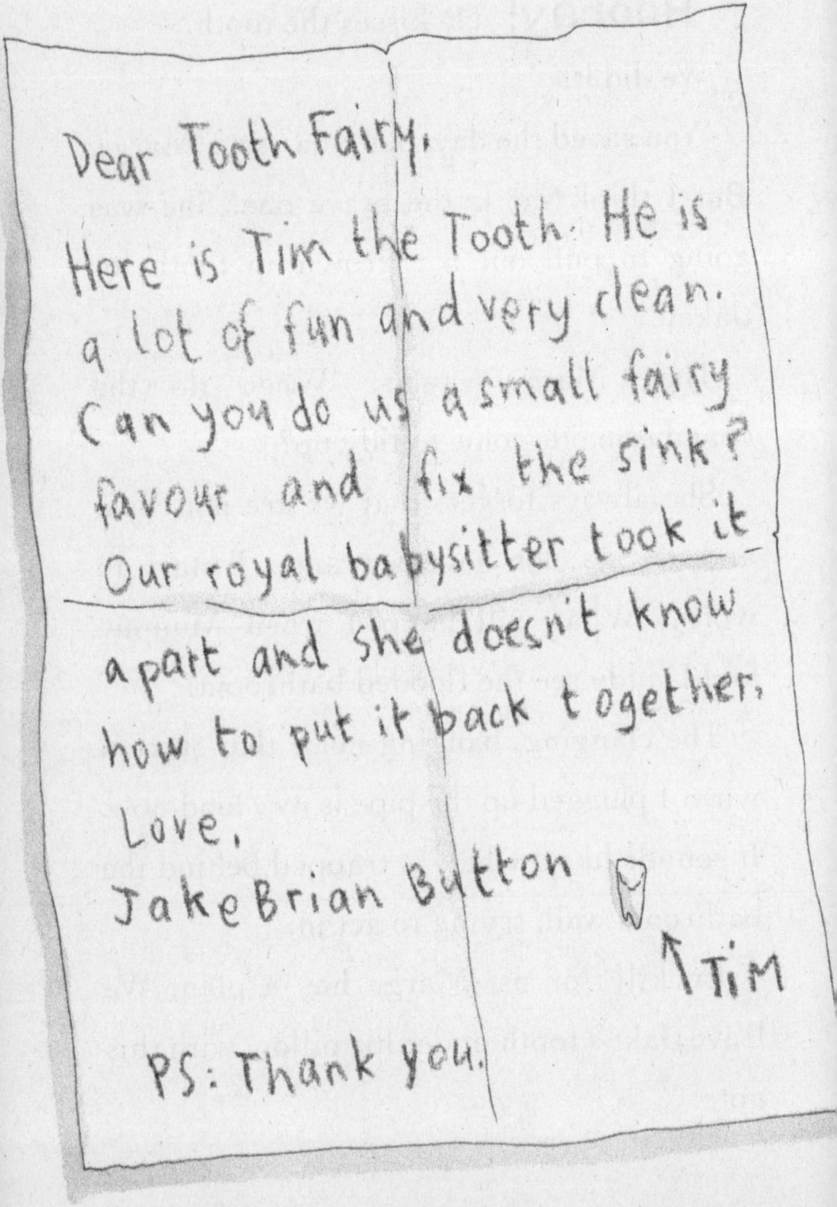

Dear Tooth Fairy,

Here is Tim the Tooth. He is
a lot of fun and very clean.
Can you do us a small fairy
favour and fix the sink?
Our royal babysitter took it
apart and she doesn't know
how to put it back together.
Love,
Jake Brian Button

↑Tim

PS: Thank you.

And would you believe that when we wake up in the morning the bathroom is spotless and there is a shiny coin under Jakey's pillow!

Marge and the Great Train Rescue

I can't believe this is actually happening to me. Two amazing things on the same day! One – Marge, the most fun grown-up on the planet, except for Mummy (and sometimes Daddy), is babysitting us. Two – Mummy has arranged a visit to the zoo and we are going by train.

A real *train*.

My belly is doing backflips. It's me, Jemima Button, and I am sitting on my bedroom floor while my brother plays with his toy train set. Jake has built a track that travels all the way from the kitchen into our bedroom and I have tripped over it twice.

'Trains go faster than cars.' Jakey lifts up his tank engine and whizzes it past my head.

'Planes go the fastest,' I remind him.

'But trains make a cool sound,' Jakey says. I kind of have to agree with him.

Jakey wants to be a train driver when he grows up. When he was little Daddy used to take him to see the 'choo choos' and he would always cry when it was time to come home. That's how much he loves trains.

DING DONG

That's our doorbell.

Whoopee!

Jakey and I scramble over each other as we run for the door, screaming so loudly that Mummy spills tea in her lap.

Marge is here. What a sight to see!

Marge is so small that she could be a hobbit. She even told us that once Santa Claus mistook her for an elf and asked her to help him deliver Christmas presents.

This morning Marge is wearing a long pink furry scarf that trails all the way down her back and a spotted pink sun hat. She looks kind of like a pink flamingo but with shorter legs.

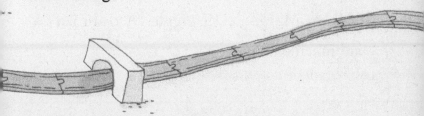

'Jolly jumbucks!' she hoots, pulling three silver train tickets out of her backpack. 'We three musketeers are off on an adventure.'

She takes our hands and we all skip in a circle, shrieking.

'Hi, Marge,' Mummy says, wiping brown tea off her trousers. 'The train leaves at nine o'clock and the station isn't far.'

While Marge consults her pocket watch, I give Mummy a hug because I don't want her to feel left out by how pleased we are to see Marge.

'We must dash,' Marge announces. 'We need to be the first ones to board the train, you see. Then we can ride at the front with the admiral and look out the window at the fish when we go underwater.'

'Um, Marge . . .' I giggle. 'A train isn't a submarine.'

'You mean, trains don't go under the sea?'
Marge squints.

Mummy laughs. Our babysitter can be so
silly.

'They do go under the sea, but inside a
tunnel,' I explain.

Marge looks surprised but not entirely
convinced.

'Have fun on the train and enjoy the zoo,
kiddos.' Mummy gives us each a brown
paper bag with cucumber sandwiches inside.

'Please make sure Jakey doesn't only eat
the bread,' Mummy says, and Jakey rolls his
eyes.

My little brother has two rules:

1. When he is eating a sandwich,
he only eats the bread. It doesn't
matter what the filling is - he
won't eat it EVER. Even if it's
jam.

2. Jakey won't stand in line. He hates being 'patient' and says patience is stupid.

'And remember, kids, Marge is in charge.' Mummy kisses us goodbye.

It's only once we have started the walk to the station that I notice Marge is carrying two large suitcases as well as her backpack.

ROLL ROLL

'I never leave the palace without my hat collection. It could rain or shine or we might get invited to tea and scones,' Marge pants, dragging everything behind her.

I think Marge has lots of hats because she needs to hide her hair. Have I told you about Marge's hair? Our babysitter has the coolest red, green, yellow, orange and blue hair. But she doesn't ever show it to grown-ups. Only we know her secret. I'm not sure Mummy and Daddy would let Marge look after us if they saw her crazy hair or knew she has a long-tooth ferret called Bert who she trained to play the harmonica.

The train station is very busy with people scurrying this way and that. There is a big board with all the places the trains go to on it. Marge is staring at the board, and at our tickets. She looks confused.

'Platform three hundred and ninety-one,' she announces after a long time.

I look over the edge of the railing and count the shiny trains and platforms beneath us. That doesn't sound right so I take our tickets.

'That's coach 3, seat number 91," I say as I look carefully at the board. 'We need to go to platform one.'

Marge is the kind of babysitter that you sometimes have to babysit, if you get what I mean. I think it's because she grew up in a palace where she had lots of nannies, a cook and a butler to do things for her.

The platform is crammed with people, and Jakey and I hold hands because we don't want to be swept away.

TOOT TOOT

A big red train chugs down the track towards us. Jakey is grinning with all his teeth as we join the queue to board.

'You broke your own rule,' I tease my brother. 'You are waiting in a line.'

'This isn't a line. It's a squiggle.' Jakey is so stubborn.

We don't get far before Marge realises that somehow on the short ride down the escalator she has lost our tickets – or 'misplaced' them, as she calls it. Luckily I am very good at finding things. Over the past year I have found Daddy's reading glasses five times, Mummy's missing glove and I even found a coin in the crack of a pavement.

'Look!' I spy them poking out from under her hat.

'Who put them up there? That's very odd.' Marge eyes the crowd suspiciously. Jakey and I pretend to be curious but we both know Marge must have just forgotten putting them there.

'You know, I am very handy on a train,' Marge tells us. 'You might say I'm an expert. When I used to ride the Queen's carriage, the King would call me Mechanical Marge.' Marge is chatting as we scramble on excitedly. 'This type of train is called a high-speed monorail and it has wings so it can fly over mountains too.'

Someone else is listening to our train expert.

'Nonsense!' says a bald man in a blue

uniform. 'A train isn't an aeroplane!' His name tag says HAROLD.

Jakey is staring at his head, 'Who are you and what happened to your hair?'

'I am the conductor. Now move on back as we are leaving shortly,' Harold scolds us.

The train looks much bigger on the inside. There is carpet on the floor and all the seats are numbered so it's not hard to find where we are meant to be. I race to sit by the window. Jakey sits next to me and once Marge has heaved her suitcases onto the shelf above us, she sits opposite. Every time I think about how fast the train will go my tummy feels kind of weird and tingly.

'The royal train has a special carriage for pet grooming. I used to take my albino water buffalo to have his tail washed and –' Marge begins.

Before she can finish her sentence a voice
booms over the loudspeaker.

'Attention, passengers, the train is about
to depart. Please stand clear of the closing
doors.'

There is a gentle HUM as the train slides
out of the station and gathers speed.

'Look!' Jakey points out the window at the trees and buildings whizzing past. 'We are going so fast.'

We *are* going way faster than when I ride my bike and a lot faster then the tallest slide at school. I am definitely feeling nervous until Marge begins to sing in her warbly voice.

'It doesn't fly in the air
Or swim though the sea,
It's longer than a car,
And slower than a star,
It keeps you dry in the rain,
It's not a coat . . . it's a train.'

Again a voice comes over the loudspeaker:

'Good afternoon, my name is Gerard and I am your train driver for the day. We expect no delays.'

'Please can I drive the train?' Jakey begs.

'Of course.' Marge pats his head.

You know how grown-ups always say that something is going to happen and it doesn't? Like when Daddy says he will water Mummy's plants or Mummy says that we can go on the fun ride outside the supermarket? Marge never does that. If Marge says Jakey will drive the train, he will. I am just not sure how safe that will be for the other passengers.

'Come on then, let's find Gerard, the driver.' Marge stands up and we make our way through the carriages towards the front of the train.

Trying to walk on a moving train is a bit like trying to stand up on a swing.

We keep losing our balance and having to grab on to things. At one point, I fall on top of a lady who is sleeping in her seat. Thankfully she doesn't wake up, but Jakey gets the giggles.

Finally we reach the glass doors that lead to where the driver sits. Marge is about to slide them open when we hear a stern voice.

'Stop in the name of railroad safety.'

We turn to see Harold again.

'Exactly what do you think you are doing?' he demands.

Marge curtsies.

'My name is Margery Beauregard Victoria Pontefois and I am a duchess. We have a request for the driver.'

'NO ONE except the driver is allowed *inside* the driver's cabin. Not even a duchess,' Harold states.

'But how can Jakey drive the train from *outside* the driver's cabin?' Marge asks.

Harold's face is a little bit like a balloon that's having too much air pushed into it.

'Drive the train?' His face is going from red to purple. 'This child doesn't even have a licence! Have you lost your marbles?!'

'No, but I did lose our train tickets for a moment. Thankfully Jemima found them inside my hat.' Marge smiles.

Harold's eyebrows are sliding off his face in fury. 'Passengers never drive the train!!'

'Jakey has had a lot of practice driving his toy trains actually, so there's no need to be afraid,' Marge replies.

'I am not afraid of anything!' He sniffs. 'Not of the dark or spiders or even loud thunder.

And I'm definitely not afraid of three small children!' He marches us back to our seats.

'But I'm a grown-up,' Marge corrects him.

'Then you should know better. A child? Driving a train? What's next, a monkey flying a spacecraft?!'

'Actually the first animal in space was a monkey named Albert,' Marge tells him.

'Nonsense!' Harold stomps off.

We all slide glumly into our seats. I can see Jakey's eyes are filling with water.

I feel sad too. For a moment I thought that Jakey was going to get to drive the train. It would have made him so happy and been such a brilliant story to tell our friends.

But Marge already has a plan. We are going to wear disguises! Marge calls this going 'undercover' and it means we can sneak our way back to the driver's cabin without Harold catching us.

Our babysitter's eyes twinkle as she pulls down her suitcases.

Marge finds a blue trilby hat for Jakey. 'Your spy name is Jake Bond.' She plonks a navy-blue beret (which is a fancy hat that French people wear) on my head. 'Your spy name is Sneaky Baguette.'

Finally she finds a furry cap for herself. 'And I shall be known as Stealthy Squirrel.'

Next she finds sunglasses for us all.

'Harold will still see that it is us,' I worry.

But no one listens to me. 'Marge is in charge!' Jakey grins.

Just as we are about to set off on the mission Marge remembers something.

'We need to wear gloves,' she says, hunting through her suitcase, 'so we don't leave any fingerprints.'

It turns out Marge doesn't have any gloves
so she suggests we wear socks on our hands
instead. It feels a bit strange (and itchy)
wearing sock mittens. Marge decides that
we may have to split up if we are spotted. 'I
don't want to split up!' Jakey looks scared
for a second. 'That bald man is very strict.'

Because he is so brave, it's easy to forget

that my little brother is only four years old.

'Don't worry, Jake Bond. Sneaky Baguette and Stealthy Squirrel will stay with you!' I say, giving him a snuggle.

We move swiftly through the carriage, trying to not make eye contact with anyone or lose our balance. My beret keeps slipping over one eye and we are getting strange looks from people. Jakey's polkadot 'gloves' are too big and come up to his elbows. He looks half boy, half dalmation puppy.

Just as we are almost at the front of the train, we spy Harold collecting tickets.

'Hide!' Jakey yelps, as he pulls us into the toilet and locks the door.

This room is too small for three people. We are all squashed together like toes in a slipper. Above the sound of the engine we can hear footsteps and chatter.

Jakey slides the door open and takes a peek. 'The coast is clear!'

We make a dash for it, huffing and puffing up the last bit of the carriage. We are about to go into the driver's cabin when

SCREEEEEECCHHHH!!!

There is a piercing sound followed by the hiss of the brakes and we tumble forward as the train grinds to a STOP.

Gerard's voice comes over the loudspeaker again. 'Sorry for the delay. It appears that we have a problem on the track.'

'I'm never going to drive the train now it's broken!' Jakey pouts.

'Mechanical Marge to the rescue,' Marge cries.

We peer out of the window, looking for

a clue. All I can see are trees and a water tower and a car on a faraway road. Jakey runs to the other side of the train to get a different view. I hope that we are not stuck for too long.

'I think the twin engine and the hover blades have sprung a leak,' Marge concludes.

'LOOK!' I say. There, standing on the tracks and looking very relaxed, is a big brown ... COW!

Harold is pacing up and down and doesn't seem to have noticed that we have snuck our way back *or* that we are wearing silly hats.

He faces us and all the passengers. 'As you can see, there is a wild and vicious beast blocking our path and only when it moves on can we continue with our journey.'

Wild and vicious? I am confused. I stare more closely. There is green grass all over the tracks and the cow is chomping happily. 'That cow might never move on,' I say. 'The zoo will be closed by the time we get there.'

'We'll just have to wait,' Harold warns. 'It's not safe for anyone to go out there. That monster could tear our limbs from our body. It could eat us alive and trample our bones!'

I shake my head. Poor Harold must be scared of cows.

'I've never heard of a killer cow,' Jakey whispers to Marge.

'I have,' Marge whispers back. 'But that's another story.'

Then she looks at Harold. 'I thought you weren't afraid of anything,' she reminds him.

'I thought so too . . . until I saw that hairy scary monster cow!' He starts to sob.

Marge places a socked hand on Harold's shoulder. 'Would you like us to help?' she asks. 'I am incredibly fond of cattle. I once dressed up my pet cow Annabella as a ballerina and taught her to pirouette.'

Learning to pirouette: grace embodied. ♥

Harold nods in relief. 'Yes, please.'

And that's how Jakey, Marge and I find ourselves on the edge of the tracks, just a few minutes later, heading towards the cow.

Marge makes a weird clicking sound with her tongue and claps her hands. The cow stares at us as Marge rummages inside her backpack and pulls out our cucumber sandwiches.

Oh no. Mummy won't like this one bit. Marge is giving our lunch away to stray animals!

'*Yassou* is Greek for "hello" and, as I suspected, this is a Greek cow,' Marge tells us as she stops and gets down on all fours and MOOS at the cow.

The cow's ears flick backwards and forwards like the windscreen wipers on

a car. Slowly she starts walking towards Marge and then turns to me.

Oh my goodness. Why has this cow picked me? I don't speak Greek. Marge passes me a sandwich and I hold it out to the cow, who is getting closer and closer. She has round curious eyes fringed with long eyelashes. My hand starts to shake a little as the cow lowers her head. I can feel hot breath and whiskers tickling my palm as she takes the sandwich inside her lips. She chews for a moment and then spits out the cucumber.

'I told you, Jemima,' Jakey whispers, being careful not to startle her. 'Even cows like only the bread!'

I can't believe it! I am feeding a cow. I let my palm touch the velvety fur on her nose. It's so soft.

Marge looks on proudly. Then she stands up and makes the clicking sound again. And would you believe that the cow starts following her? Marge, Jakey and I lead the animal off the tracks and over to where the rest of the herd is standing by the trees.

I am puffed up with pride as I high-five Jakey and Marge. We did it!

Back aboard, the rest of the passengers give us three cheers.

Harold looks very relieved. 'Would you like to come and meet the driver?' he offers.

Jakey is so thrilled that he blows an underarm raspberry. He only does this when something is incredibly exciting, like the time he found the face paints after Mummy had hidden them.

Gerard, the driver, has a bushy moustache and seems delighted to have visitors. Particularly ones who have helped him keep his train on schedule.

He shakes our hands, 'You must be the Cattle Herders who saved the day. Welcome!'

Jakey and I can't believe how many buttons there are in the driver's cab. Gerard shows us the brake and throttle controls. We see a big blue computer screen with control-indicator lights and another panel that reads 'fuel system'. Jakey pulls the horn.

TOOT TOOT

It must all be too much for Marge, because while Gerard is explaining what everything does, she gives a big yawn.

'You know, Greek cows are very friendly by nature, not like Spanish cows,' Marge murmurs as she curls up in the corner.

Her furry cap is still on and her little legs are poking out as she promptly falls fast asleep.

Now, what happens next is the most amazing thing ever, even more amazing than all the incredible animals that we will get to see later . . .

Finally Jakey is allowed to hold the throttle!

I get a lump in my throat as I watch. His little tongue is poking out in concentration and he looks so proud of himself! I can't wait to tell Daddy that Jakey drove the train.

Then, can you believe it, I get a turn too.

I can't do a forward roll yet or click my fingers . . . but I, Jemima Button The Cattle Herder, can drive a train!

Marge and the Zany Zoo Day

It's me again, Jemima Button, and I have great news – we made it to the zoo!

On our long walk from the train station Marge sang a silly song that gave Jakey and me the giggles.

'There's no place like the zoo,
You can ride on a kangaroo,
You can feed a crocodile too,
Just don't step in animal-poo.'

We have had such a fantastic day already and now we get to see all our favourite animals!

'I can't wait to see Oliver the Orangutan!'

My little brother is jumping over the cracks in the pavement.

Oliver the Orangutan is the reason Jakey loves the zoo. He's so big and furry and he sort of acts like a human. He and Jakey are best zoo friends: last time we came here they

had a dance-off. Whatever my brother did, the orangutan would copy him. Even the zookeeper was laughing. But when Jakey took a turn at following Oliver, it all went wrong.

The orangutan turned his bum to everyone and started flinging his poop at the glass.

That's when Mummy decided it was time to leave. We haven't been back to the zoo since, until today!

We join the queue of people at the entrance. I don't even mind waiting to get inside because I am so excited. Marge has let me look after the money for our tickets. I feel like such a big girl!

Did I tell you that I am doing a project in school on chameleons? They are a kind of lizard that can change colour. I have brought all of my coloured pencils (because I don't know which colour the chameleon will be today) and I am going to sketch one.

The line is moving very slowly. 'Look, I can see the giraffes from here!' I point at where two giraffes are looking over the zoo fence and chewing slowly, their long purple tongues slipping out to catch stray grass.

Jakey and I watch them for a minute, before I realise things have gone strangely quiet.

We turn back and Marge is nowhere to be seen.

'**Marge?!**' I call out.

'**Marge?!**' Jakey repeats.

But there is no answer. Where has she gone? We walk through the queue shouting loudly.

'**Marge! Here, Marge!**' says Jakey.

'Have you lost your dog?' asks one lady very kindly.

'No,' I tell her, 'we've lost our babysitter.'

'Have you seen her?' Jakey asks. 'She's about this tall –' he holds his hand up to my forehead '– and she has rainbow hair and she looks like an Oompa-Loompa from *Charlie and the Chocolate Factory*.'

The lady looks at us strangely, but just

then I spy Marge way up ahead of us. She's wearing sunglasses and crawling along the ground towards the ticket gates!

'Pardon me,' I cry as Jakey and I race to the front of the line. Ahead of us, Marge crawls between the legs of the man selling tickets, slides past the gates and ducks behind a bush. She's inside the zoo and no one is stopping her!

We try to follow but the man at the gate stops us.

'Is there a grown-up with you?' he asks. 'Children can't enter the zoo alone.'

'Um, yes ... she went, er, ahead of us,' I stammer.

He doesn't look as if he believes me, so I hand over the money that Marge gave us.

He studies us for a minute, tips his zoo worker hat and waves us though. He even gives us free tokens for animal food.

Phew, we are in!

Marge pops out from behind a bush.

'Marge, you didn't pay for a ticket!' I scold her.

'I have a pass for the full year,' Marge says, slipping her shades off. She shows it to us proudly.

'Then why did you sneak in?' I ask. I am confused.

'I'm not technically allowed back in the zoo after last time,' Marge confesses in a whisper.

'What happened the last time?' Jakey's eyes are as round as golf balls.

I am not quite sure I want to know the answer. Whatever it is, Mummy wouldn't like it.

'Last time I was here,' Marge admits, 'I accidentally opened some cages and set a few of the animals free. I released Grace the Warthog – she looked so glum! Then I freed Sam the Lion, or as I named him, Sad-Sam-Stuck-in-His-Cage.' Marge looks embarrassed. 'But freedom has its price.

All the zoo visitors were screaming!

Then the zookeepers organised a big search. Eventually we found Sam and Grace.

Sam was snoozing in the butterfly house.

Grace was in the cafeteria, helping herself to hot dogs.

So it was all absolutely hunky-dory, but the head zookeeper told me that I'd better not come back.'

Jakey looks as happy as can be. 'Let's let Oliver the Orangutan free so he can come home with us!' he begs.

That is the worst idea ever! I share a bedroom with Jake and it already looks like a giant mess *before* an orangutan moves in.

We open up a map of the zoo. 'Well, young explorers,' says Marge, 'where shall we go first?'

'Let's see Oliver the Orangutan,' Jakey cries.

'I think we should see the baby tigers first,' I suggest. Oliver is all the way at the bottom of the map and there are amazing animals nearby that can't be missed. Marge agrees and off we go. I feel like skipping, so I do. Marge and Jakey join in and we decide that's how we will get around the zoo.

The Tiger Enclosure is massive and it takes us a while to spot the babies. There are two of them and a sign tells us that the cubs are now six months old.

'That's about your age in tiger years, Jemima,' says Marge, watching them. 'You know, I spent some time travelling with the circus years ago. They called me a tiger-whisperer, because I speak tiger. And I'm very good at whispering.'

Marge shows us how to whisper to the tigers, but the cubs are busy playing together, chasing a rubber ball. They don't seem to be very good at listening. Maybe we are not whispering about the right things. I try to think of interesting secrets to tell the baby tigers. Like that I used to believe that stuffed animals came alive when I went to sleep, or that getting new shoes made you run faster.

Our whispering gets louder and louder and everyone at the Tiger Enclosure is staring at us *except* for the tigers. Then Marge starts hissing and growling at them! Now the cubs pay attention. They both freeze, whimper and dart into their little cave.

Marge has scared them away! The zookeeper looks cross as he heads towards us.

'Let's move along,' says Marge in one last whisper.

We have barely continued our journey before my brother pipes up again.

'Now can we see Oliver the Orangutan?'

I tell him that we have a few other animals to see first and he has to learn patience. We say hi to the elephants and spy on the hippos having a bath. We wave at the zebras and show the flamingos how we can stand on one leg too.

When we arrive at the Penguin Habitat, we sit in a small crowd and watch a zookeeper throwing slimy fish to the penguins.

'Who wants to feed them some mackerel?' the zookeeper asks. All of the children put their hands up, but Marge is the only adult who does.

'Ooooh, ooooh, pick me please, me, me!' Marge shouts.

'Are you a child or a grown-up?' the zookeeper asks.

'A grown-up! Please pick her,' Jakey says, jumping up and down.

The zookeeper hands Marge the bucket of fish. Marge picks up an extra-slimy one and holds it in the air. The penguins are flapping around excitedly.

Then Marge holds the fish up even higher above her head, opens her mouth and drops the slippery fish straight in! I don't know who gasps louder, the people or the penguins.

'Ah, I love mackerel,' says Marge. 'So good for you too. All those healthy fish oils.'

The penguins and the people stare at her.

'Jakey, Jemima – fancy a treat?' I shake my head firmly. A wet fish is not a treat – **YUCK!**

To everyone's horror, Marge gulps down a few more fish. Then she carefully places two in her backpack for later and feeds the rest to the penguins, who still look a bit annoyed with her.

'After that delicious lunch,' she tells Jake and me as we leave the Penguin Habitat, 'it's time for ice cream!'

While I am having a Strawberry Creamsickle and Jakey is eating four scoops of mint chocolate chip, I look at the map again.

We're very close to the Petting Zoo, which is one of the most fun things to do. Jakey and I use our tokens to buy food. Now that we are experienced cattle herders we feel very sure of ourselves around the cows, ducks, sheep and goats.

Marge perches on a rock in the middle of

the park and all the animals surround us.

Jakey and I feed them and pet them. One of the cows is brown all over and I can't help wishing she could make chocolate milk instead of regular.

She keeps rubbing her head on my back. I want to show Marge, but she has her hands full.

She is holding a goat in her arms like a baby, covering it with kisses while singing a lullaby!

Then she kisses a duck, straight on its beak. She does the same with all the sheep too, even the ones that run away. She just chases them down until she catches them and lays a giant smooch on their dusty, dirty sheep noses. Marge loves animals more than anyone I know!

As we are leaving the Petting Zoo, the keeper shows us where to wash our hands.

'You might want to wash your mouth too,' he advises Marge.

'*Now* can we go to Oliver the Orangutan?' says Jakey, hopping from foot to foot. 'I've waited *ages*.'

'Soon, Jakey,' I tell him. I have found the Reptile and Insect House on the map, where I am pretty sure the chameleon lives. I point it out to Marge and we all skip off.

It's dark and damp in the Reptile and Insect House, and I have to blink a few times to see the displays. Jakey takes my hand and we walk over to the first glass enclosure.

Straightaway Marge spots Katie the Chameleon. She's bright green and scaly and clinging to a rock.

I take out my pencils to start drawing her. She's so still and doesn't move an inch. I wait for a more dramatic pose.

Jakey starts getting fidgety and moves on.

'Look in this window!' he gulps.

I race over to where he is.

It's dark, but lit with a small orange light. There are some branches and rocks inside and a . . . furry-legged, big-headed, tarantula spider!

'**Arrghh!**' Marge shrieks, '**HELP! SPIDER!**'

She jumps onto my back and clings on like superglue.

'We are in the Insect House – of course there are spiders!' I say. 'Although actually, spiders are not insects. They are arachnids.' But Marge doesn't seem to be listening and everyone is staring at us. I am giving a grown-up a piggyback!

'It's going to attack me!' Marge continues.

She is surprisingly not very heavy for a grown-up.

'It's behind the glass!' I try to calm her.

'Surely it could smash the glass with its pointy poisonous fangs!' Marge panics.

'That one isn't even venomous,' I say,

moving closer to read what's written about it, forgetting Marge is now closer to the spider too.

'**Arrgghh!**' Marge screams as loudly as she can. Then, as if the whole building is on fire, she leaps off my back and jumps over a baby in his pram, landing on the ground with a bump. Still terrified, she springs up and dives through a whole class of schoolchildren, pushing their teacher aside and elbowing a grandfather on her way out.

When Jakey and I find her she is still trembling in fear.

'When I lived in the palace the king had every one of those beastly creepy-crawlies captured and banished to another kingdom.'

I am so surprised. I always imagined that Marge loved all creatures, even slugs.

'But we have to go back inside. I need to finish my drawing,' I say.

Before Marge can answer, a voice booms over the loudspeaker.

'Come one, come all, to the Birds of Paradise Aviary Show, happening right now in Parrot Cove!'

Marge claps her hands gleefully.

'I *love* parrots. I had one once called Lady Biscuit, but she fell in love with a badger and eloped.'

'When are we going to see Oliver the Orangutan?' Jakey whines.

'Next, I promise,' I tell my little brother. 'I still have to finish my school project.'

We check the zoo map and skip our way to Parrot Cove. We take a seat in the front. Birds the colour of Marge's hair are swooshing through the air back and forth. They are so beautiful!

A hawk flaps past, collects a ring and returns it.

SOAR

A parrot chatters away.
A rainbow lorikeet
sails over our heads.
We all cheer.

SQUAWK

SWOOP

Once the show is over Marge removes a bag of seed from her backpack and pours it into a little pile on her head.

'Stay quiet and don't move,' she tells us, and sure enough all the birds start flying around and some of them are landing on Marge's head and snacking. It's wonderful to see them so close, particularly the snowy owl, who looks like a little old man with reading glasses on.

'Now can we go to Oliver the Orangutan?' Jakey nags.

'Now can we go to Oliver the Orangutan?' a red parrot repeats.

'Now can we go to Oliver the Orangutan,' squawks another yellow parrot.

Soon a green one chips in and then a blue and they are all chorusing:

'Now can we go to Oliver the Orangutan?'

It is *really* starting to annoy me, I feel like it's the only sentence I have heard all day. I am just about to tell Jakey off when I see something white and sticky whizzing by me. It lands on Marge's head!

It takes me a second to realise what is happening as another dollop flies down and lands with a **PLOP** on my shoulder. *Oh no!* The birds are pooping. Another load drops with a **SPLAT** on Jakey's head.

'EWWW, RUN!' I yell.

'Getting pooped on is good luck!' Marge puffs as we make a dash to the bathroom, 'Chester my Meerkat once pooped on my foot during a game of hide-and-seek and sure enough I was never found!'

A BLESSING IN DISGUISE.

We clean ourselves up with wet wipes and then at last we skip off to see Oliver the Orangutan. Even though he is driving me crazy, I know how much my little brother has been looking forward to this so I don't want anything to spoil it.

But would you believe what happens next? As we get close, we notice that the whole area where Oliver lives is empty!

He's not on the rope swing, he's not lying on his netting hammock and he is not up his favourite tree. Poor Jakey starts to panic.

I suddenly see a big sign and read it aloud.

OLIVER IS VISITING THE VET.
HE WILL BE BACK NEXT WEDNESDAY.

Jakey's face is crumbling. My little brother has two rules:

1. He always wears his welly boots in summer and sandals in the winter.

2. He only goes to the zoo to see Oliver the Orangutan.

Jakey's shoulders sag and his bottom lip is wobbling. I feel so badly for him. He is starting to cry and I can tell he is going to howl. A whole other class of children have arrived and seem just as disappointed.

'I want to see Oliver,' wails a girl in pigtails.

I give my little brother a huge hug, but then I realise that Marge is missing again. I can't believe that Mummy told Marge to keep an eye on us, but it us who should be keeping an eye on Marge!

'Ohh aahhh oooh ahhh!'

We turn in surprise. A grunting sound is coming from the corner of the cage. Then we see some rustling in a bush inside Oliver's enclosure.

'Look,' the teacher announces to her group of schoolchildren. 'What's that?'

'Oliver must be back from the vet!' I feel so relieved as I grin at Jakey.

But it's *Marge* who pops her head out of the bush!

She is wearing an orange hat and thumping her chest. To be honest she looks more like a traffic cone than an orangutan, but no one seems to mind.

Marge swings from
rope to rope,

then she shrieks as
she grooms herself,

before she runs
to the glass and
beats it exactly
like Oliver does.

There is such a commotion that the zookeeper comes to investigate. He looks extremely angry, but just then a bigger crowd of children starts to appear. They are clapping and cheering and no one minds at all that it isn't the real Oliver.

Jakey shuffles forward and starts playing with Marge like he usually does with Oliver.

He shakes his head 'no' and Marge copies him. Then he starts laughing and Marge mimics him too.

Marge is even better than Oliver at being an orangutan.

Jakey is so happy and so am I – but I haven't even told you the best part yet.

After Marge's show, the zookeeper lets me meet Katie the Chameleon up close.

She has a long curly tail and, when Marge puts her on top of her head, she turns all the colours of the rainbow. I finally get to sketch her and I use every single one of my coloured pencils!

Jakey and I look at each other and share a secret smile. We truly have the best babysitter in the world!

ISLA FISHER
Bestselling Author
Marge
and the

AUSTRALIA

Secret Tunnel

'Charming, funny, delightful' *DAVID BADDIEL*

ZOOM! WHIZZ!
Marge is on the move!

Life with Marge is NEVER boring!
She has rainbow hair,
goes skiing in summer
and is the best babysitter
you could wish for.

And maybe – just maybe –
Marge can help Jemima and Jakey
find out who (or what) is at the
other end of the secret tunnel.

PRESS

Thank you for choosing a Piccadilly Press book.

If you would like to know more about our authors, our books or if you'd just like to know what we're up to, you can find us online.

www.piccadillypress.co.uk

You can also find us on:

We hope to see you soon!